Praise for

Dodging Satan: My Irish/Italian, Sometimes Awesome, but Mostly Creepy, Childhood has won two CIPA EVVY Awards--First Place in Religion and Spirituality and Second Place winner in Humor; the Bronze Illumination Award, the e-Lit Award, and was a 2016 Finalist in Humor for Foreword Review's Book of the Year.

A girl, roiled by emergent sexuality, conflicting emotions toward parents, an extended family of abusive men and unhappy women: the protagonist in this playful but gripping tale draws on a hilarious mishmash of Catholic popular culture, creating outrageous cosmic narratives to make sense of it all. Catholics will recognize it; those who didn't have access to the Catholic Imagination while growing up will be jealous.

Michael P. Carroll
Madonnas that Maim
Catholic Cults and Devotions
The Cult of the Virgin Mary

Tender and ruthlessly honest, Kathleen McCormick's beautiful first novel draws us into the world of Italian Irish Catholicism as experienced by its unforgettably wise and desperately innocent girl narrator. There's magic in this world--and while we are charmed by its glow, we are also unsettled again and again by the darkness behind that glow. We follow Bridget with trepidation, captivated by her vulnerability and her fierceness, trusting there's much to learn from her journey.

Edvige Giunta
Writing with an Accent; *Personal Effects*

If you want to know what spiritual bouquets are or why 'rules are so confusing here on earth,' read Kathleen McCormick's deeply perceptive and slyly voiced novel about the challenges of girlhood Catholicism and the perils of having to overcome both pride and humility through the comical harrowing of an Irish-Italian family.

George Guida
The Pope Stories and Other Tales of Troubled Times

Dodging Satan is a hilarious and heartbreaking novel of growing up in an Irish/Italian Catholic family filled with religious certainty and ethnic strife. It outdoes Mary McCarthy's *Memories of a Catholic Girlhood* in its wit, intelligence and irresistible mixture of realism and charm. It is simply a joy to read. Written in the voice of Bridget, a young girl caught between visions of Satan and sanctity, bewitched in a Catholic school that enforces ideals of the holy family and a home filled with lively, arguing relatives, it is captivating in its mixture of humor and grit. Bridget makes her way through Irish, Italian and religious patriarchies with the heart and mind of a gifted observer looking for her own form of grace. McCormick has written a brilliant work, filled with all the astonishment, allure and pitfalls of ethnic life today.

Josephine Gattuso Hendin
Vulnerable People: A View of American Fiction Since 1945
Heart Breakers: Women and Violence in Contemporary Culture
The Right Thing To Do

A coming of age feminist consciousness story that navigates gender in the contexts of domestic and celestial hierarchies. In Bridget's world, frightening and glorious relationships exist between phosphorous and holiness, virgins and bicycles, crucifixes and spices, exorcism and mascara. Zamboni-McCormick renders scenes that run the gamut from laugh-out-loud Catholic brainwashing of children, to heart-wrenched witnessing of domestic violence, to riveting teenage excursions toward sex.

Annie Rachele Lanzillotto
L is for Lion: an italian bronx butch freedom memoir

To Michele

Dodging Satan

My Irish/Italian
sometimes awesome,
but mostly creepy,
childhood

By Kathleeen Zamboni McCormick

SHRP
Sand Hill Review Press

Copyright © 2015 By Kathleen McCormick
Published by Sand Hill Review Press, LLC

www.sandhillreviewpress.com
P.O. Box 1275, San Mateo, CA 94401
(415) 297-3571

Library of Congress Control Number: 2015935929
ISBN: 978-1-937818-27-2 ebook edition, November, 2015
ISBN: 978-1-937818-32-6 paperback, February, 2016
ISBN: 978-1-937818-61-6 case laminate, July, 2017

*Dodging Satan: My Irish/Italian, sometimes awesome,
but mostly creepy, childhood* is a work of fiction. Its
characters, scenes and locales are the product of the
author's imagination or are used fictitiously. Any similarity
of fictional characters to people living or dead is purely
coincidental.

SHRP
Sand Hill Review Press

For Gary and Philip

Table of Contents

1. Why Is God in Daddy's Slippers?

The Italian and Irish sides of our family can argue about almost anything—the thickness of porridge, how much people can drink before they're officially alcoholics, and which side acts more like "bloody foreigners." But they all agree on the sacredness of the crucifix. An uncle on each side survived an attack in WWII that killed the rest of their platoons—all because they were wearing their crucifixes.

I volunteer to tell the story of the miracle of my uncles' salvation to my second grade class. The bombs were bursting in air. My uncles, years before my birth, were staring at the rockets' red glare. The rockets were about to come down on them when they touched their crosses around their necks, and God touched them back. A heavenly host of angels singing alleluia held up American flags against our enemies who didn't believe in God. And all of this to save my two uncles, Johnny Flaherty and Tony Alonzo. God is Italian. Or Irish. Either way, He was on our side. That's why we won.

Sister Helen Mary directs me me back to my desk. She won't allow my classmates to ask me any questions, even though their hands are waving frantically, and many are calling out "Ssst! Ssst!" half-standing up. It's a great story. And it's true. But Sister Helen Mary says it's time for phonics.

My mother is summoned to the principal's office soon after I've revealed what are, after all, truths about my uncles. She's commanded to return again later in the month when I illustrate my Easter alphabet book with our family's signs of war and redemption. A is for angels (and Alleluia). B is for bombs. C is for crucifix. D is for dead. Sister Helen Mary warns that I can't mention my uncles or crucifixes any more in school. I reassure her that we have a lot of family secrets, but the story of my uncles and the war isn't one of them. She won't listen. My uncles' salvation becomes a new kind of secret, a school secret. Catholic school is so disillusioning. The crucifix is clearly more sacred to my family than to the nuns, who're supposed to be God's brides, aren't they?

Sister Helen Mary wants our alphabet books to be about Easter food and Jesus and the resurrection and eternal salvation and flowers. So I take on the challenge of Easter food, but my mother prohibits me from drawing that A is for artichokes or antipasto, even though my grandmother makes the best artichokes on Easter, and they're one of my absolutely favorite foods. She says most of the nuns, like the families in the parish, are Irish and like my father probably disapprove of Italian food. But I feel that saying A is for "apples," while true alphabetically, is also kind of a lie—it isn't what A means to me. Lying is a sin. And since I'm seven and will receive my First Holy Communion in a month, I want my soul to be particularly spotless.

My mother says I'm not sinning, that I'm just learning to keep quiet and say something diplomatic, which you have to do a lot in life if you're going to get along with people, and that God only knows how she's had to. But it just seems like more secrets and more pretending, which I hate. As I practice drawing apples, with tears streaming down my cheeks, my mother confides that she has a story about something a lot more important than artichokes. I know this means a new family secret.

She moves my drawings off the table, gets me some milk, and in her most q.t. voice whispers that war isn't glorious, that it's actually really horrible. I've never heard that before. "C'n I've a straw, please?" This doesn't seem like it'll be a very interesting story after all.

"War is a terrible thing, Bridey, and not many people realize I only became devoted to God after your father's draft deferment." I've got no idea what she's talking about and start to blow bubbles into my milk. My mother grabs the straw away and tells me to concentrate. "It means he didn't have to go to war."

I'm stunned. Everyone in our family—on both sides—is so patriotic. How could my father not have been a soldier when he was young? And why was my mother happy about it, you know? "Why didn't he go to war?" I try to hide my disappointment.

"Because of his flat feet."

Feet? Feet! My father missed World War II because of his feet? I shake my foot out of my slipper and put it up on my chair so we can both see it. "Look, Mom, everyone's feet are kind of flat. It hardly seems—"

"Stop it!" she shouts. Her lip is trembling. Turns out that my father's feet are such a family secret that we can't talk about them in front of anyone. Even each other. "It embarrasses your father even though the money he earned working while everyone else was at war still supports Grandpa and Uncle Johnny downstairs."

I agree to keep my father's flat feet on the q.t., which is easy enough cuz people don't really talk much about feet. But I know my mother's wrong about war. The war not only proved to our families how special Johnny and Tony were in the eyes of God but how important the crucifix is to salvation.

And it looks like the rest of the family agrees with me. Hence the presence of the crucifix in all our households and in so many styles and sizes. Above the mantel here. Nearly always over the beds. In the kitchen above the spices. Sometimes even in the bathroom. I know as well as anyone that God works in mysterious ways, but in my opinion He and the angels could have done a better job saving my Uncle Johnny. Because of the shrapnel in Johnny's head, he gets wicked bad seizures and can't ever hold a job. He's also begun to drink enough for everyone to agree that he's an alcoholic. "Still fighting the war, always fighting the war," Grandpa says, shaking his head whenever they carry a sweating, shaking, and bluish Johnny into his room.

Why did my Uncle Tony, who lives in New York with most of my other Italian relatives, do so much better than Johnny? He has a blonde Italian wife and three big sons—all too old to seem like my cousins. Tony runs a successful grocery store on Staten Island and says you can buy corn on the cob from him that tastes like it's just come off the farm.

"More like just off the boat," my Irish Grandpa jeers. My father joins in, pointing out that Tony isn't my "real uncle" and his sons aren't my "real cousins" at all cuz Tony isn't my mother's brother. But who cares? I call all our Staten Island relations uncles or aunts or cousins even if they're my mother's or grandmother's cousins or second cousins twice removed.

It doesn't matter, know what I mean? What's important is we're all part of the same family. And Tony doesn't mind what grandpa or my father says. He survived foreigners attacking him all during the war and isn't about to let an Irishman bother him now. And he still always wears his crucifix.

One Saturday at breakfast, about a month before my First Holy Communion, trying not to gag over my diluted porridge, my mother announces that we're redecorating my room. I set my sights on a quite expensive ruffled bedspread. I pray to Mother Mary that one will show up in Filene's Basement in her favorite colors, blue and white. I implore St. Anthony to find matching curtains. I try my guardian angel for new lace dresser scarves. Their responses are mixed. I get a purple and pink bedspread that had been my Aunt Anna's. There are no ruffles. The new curtains are white. I have to keep the old dresser scarves.

But the greatest redecorating excitement for me is the anticipation of receiving my crucifix for my Holy Communion present. I've imagined the kind of cross I might be given for a long time. Whenever we go the Catholic store, even though we're never shopping for one, I head right for the crucifix aisle. Lying in bed at night or swinging on the swing set in the evening when the mosquitoes are biting, I can picture all the different styles of crucifixes and their descriptions.

There's the plain ten-inch cross, made of gold or silver—pretty, but there's no Jesus hanging on it. The mother-of-pearl crucifix has a multi-toned Jesus with most of his bones really sticking out, but at sixteen inches, it's probably too big for my bedroom. Uncle Johnny's and Uncle Tony's crucifixes are the popular soldiers' style: small, metal, and worn on a chain around the neck because you have no walls to hang a cross on in a war. Their crucifixes aren't appropriate for a young lady's bedroom.

My preference runs to a medium-sized, "authentic-detailed" heavy wooden crucifix. The crown of thorns on this cross is actually pointy and sharp, and deep-red blood drips down Christ's head.

You can see exactly where the long nails enter his hands and feet. Just looking at it gives you the feeling that you went through the whole fourteen Stations of the Cross. That you witnessed Saint Veronica wiping the blood and sweat from Christ's face. That you were there with Mary Mother Most Sorrowful on Calvary, desperate and helpless, as she watched the soldiers kill her son.

Some people we know think that a young girl might be afraid of realistic crucifixes, but I don't see why. It's one thing to be frightened by the Devil, you know? But how can an accurate depiction of Christ's blood bother anyone because we all understand that every wound of his, every bit of his suffering, helps to lessen ours here on earth. To give my mother subtle hints about my crucifix style preference, I endlessly draw images of a splintery wooden cross with a bleeding Jesus on scraps of paper while she paints and repapers my room. But she always throws my drawings away with the old pieces of wallpaper at the end of the day.

When the room is finished, my mother and father present me with an elaborately decorated gift. "This is to celebrate your First Holy Communion, Bridget," says my father, sounding official, but with a glint of pleasure in his eyes. "And at the same time as your room redecoration so that it can have a rightful place," adds my mother. It's got to be my crucifix, but I'm surprised the box is so small and light. Still, I unwrap it with reverence. This will be my Jesus, my own sacrificial lamb.

I can't believe it. Inside the box is a thin, almost transparent, white plastic crucifix on a tiny matching round stand—it couldn't even hang—with a puny silver Jesus on it. It's only about six inches high. The whole thing is smooth. No signs of blood, thorns, or nails. No sense of pain or torture. This is a baby's version of a cross. They don't even sell these in the Catholic store. I look at my parents, my face hot, my stomach clenched, and feel betrayed that they don't think I'm old enough for a real crucifix after all. But they're smiling.

"We're so proud of you, Bridget, growing up to be such a young lady now." They each hug me. Then my mother tells me I can go set up my crucifix on my new bedside table.

Only after my mother gets me into bed that night and turns out the light do I discover that the crucifix has magic powers. How could I have doubted my parents? In the dark the cross casts a Godly glow. It's as if Johnny and Tony's bombs bursting in air have been captured inside my Christ. The bright lights of war at night are shining through my crucifix, reminding me that God can appear to anyone He chooses, and I now see, in any way He wants.

This cross is giving me a vision of how He must have revealed Himself to my uncles when He intervened on their behalf against the enemy infidels. God shone in the darkness, His mighty hand reaching out to protect Uncle Johnny and Uncle Tony, as He's protecting me now. But very gradually there begins to creep over me an uncertainty as to whether I exactly like this form of protection, know what I mean?

"Bring light to soldiers in foreign lands who need you more than I do, since I'm already safe in my bed," I pray softly to my silver Jesus. The cross keeps shining. "Dear God, I thank you for your gift of light. Goodnight now." He glows on.

My hands begin to sweat. I feel like I have to go to the bathroom. In a fit of wild, irreverent passion that's perhaps like Johnny's seizures, I wish I wasn't Catholic, that my family were pagans and worshipped the sun, which leaves you alone at night to get some sleep. These sacrilegious thoughts still don't make the light of the cross go out. Finally I cover the crucifix with one of my pillows. I sleep fitfully, but in the morning the light has gone out. I'm so relieved. But the glow comes on again every night once it gets dark, and every night I put a pillow over the crucifix.

As my father's birthday nears, and the days get longer and warmer, God's shining out at me through my crucifix bothers me less. My mother is so excited about her special birthday present for him that it seems like he'll never get home from work to open it. Finally we gather in the living room as he unwraps his secret gift.

Slippers.

The whole family, even Grandpa, who doesn't go in much for presents anyway, is disappointed, given the fuss my mother's been making.

"Wait," she cries, seeing our expressions. "They're the latest!" pointing to the inner soles. "Dad will never lose these slippers getting out of bed at night, but you have to wait 'til it's dark to see how they work." That'll be at least another hour.

The instant the sun goes down, my mother takes the slippers from the box and tells us to have a good look inside them. They're glowing. Just like the crucifix. I think I'm going to be sick. God is in my daddy's slippers.

The more my father wears those slippers, the more I despise them cuz God, in a sneaky sort of way, can now move all around the house. If my father sits down at the kitchen table with me to have a piece of toast in the morning, God is right under the table, possibly looking up my nightie, so I have to make extra sure to keep my ankles crossed.

We're eating popcorn, enjoying the Red Sox, even though they're always losing. When my father falls asleep, off comes a slipper and there's God staring straight at me. Then I get the German

measles. My father's reading to me in my room—
Cinderella or *Diana and the Golden Apples,* two of
my favorites. He crosses one leg over the other and
slaps a slipper up and down, and God peeks out
again and again. I can't believe that God is such a
Nosey Parker.

But the more I think, the odder it seems that
God's in those slippers. I know Jesus washed the
feet of his disciples, but He didn't move into their
shoes. Sometimes my father's feet smell like Asiago.
My mother says they reek more in his slippers.
Would God want to be with stinky feet? Though just
as I'm having these doubts, the Gospel at Mass is
about God's humility. Seems he was always going
among the least of His servants. And I think of how
God chose to have His angels save Johnny and Tony
and how my father didn't get to go to war because of
his flat feet. Could these slippers be God's way—on
the q.t. of course—of telling my father it's okay he
didn't fight in the war, that his feet, though flat, are
still special?

I stop putting the pillow over my crucifix at
night. I praise Jesus for loving my father and his
feet. I thank Him for my mother, who literally
makes His light shine among us. For Father's Day,
my mother and I buy my dad a metal crucifix that
looks just like Johnny's and Tony's, and he puts it
on because I ask him to, even though he doesn't like
things around his neck. I even tell my guardian
angel it's okay about not getting the dresser scarves.

It was at least a year before I found out that
phosphorus is a chemical that makes things glow in
the dark and probably has nothing whatsoever to do
with God, salvation, the rockets' red glare, or
anything holy at all. That it's used in all sorts of
things, from crucifixes to slipper liners to Halloween
decorations. It was a number of years before I
realized that some of those foreigners my uncles

fought in the war were Italian. Real Italians. From Italy. That God doesn't have a nationality. That in some other people's eyes, we were the enemy.

But this year, my second grade class wins the school prize for buying the most pagan babies: seventy-two! I start going to morning Mass with my mother in the summer. Before swimming lessons. Tony's store continues to prosper. Uncle Johnny gets a new medicine that reduces his seizures a bit. My mother redecorates the dining room to cover up a stain on the wallpaper where she'd thrown a freshly made, hot blueberry pie at my father. And missed. My father wears his slippers every night and on the weekends. God is in our apartment this year, and all is right with the world. And no one was to know that, within a decade, two of Tony's sons, my cousins Alberto and Domenico, would come home in body bags from Vietnam—still wearing their crucifixes.

2. Satan Is in My Bedroom and Nobody Seems to Care

Having a divine presence in my bedroom wasn't a new event for me when Jesus arrived on His glow-in-the-dark crucifix or when God appeared in daddy's slippers. Though frightening, they were, at least, forces for good. Satan was the really scary one. I turned three and my crib disappeared. Sleeping was supposed to happen in a new, deep, mysterious double bed. That was when Satan, with dead glassy eyes, began visiting my bedroom every night. And so many snakes, curled like long, Christmas-present ribbons, hissing like steaming radiators, came with him.

Satan's bedtime stories slide along my walls— thick, nightmare versions of the Bible. Why is he here—in our old, brown, three-family house in Cambridge, Massachusetts—and not in hell where he belongs? His stories are like fog on a rainy night when hidden gates unlatch and bang and bang and bang insistently in the wind. There is no sleepiness in this new bed.

In the stories Satan scribbles in my mind, God-the-Father becomes so wicked that I hate Him. And any minute now I might have to give my soul away, just to stop Satan. 'Course then I'd be lost for all eternity. Satan is so sly, keeping it all on the q.t. He doesn't appear in any room but mine.

And my parents don't care, whatever I say. He consumes them with other matters. Like whether my Italian mother is an uppity guinea cuz she wants a leather handbag, even one from Filene's Basement. Or why we have to eat T-bone steaks whenever they're on sale, since my mother and I both hate red meat—gristly and slimy with animal bones imbedded, like something never meant to be chewed and swallowed. Or how my mother feels belittled by the way my Irish father treats her in front of their friends. She's always threatening to leave him.

What would happen to me without my mother? Satan doesn't let her think about that. But he makes me worry all the time about not having her anymore. Then for a while it's okay. My mother says she can't leave because she doesn't know how to drive.

"Why aren't driving lessons ever an option for you, Elda?" asks Aunt Anna, my mother's oldest sister.

And my mother goes through the roof.

The other day she started coughing after she and my father yelled, and cups and forks soared through the air like crows diving for the bread my mother throws out for the sparrows, and there was breaking and screaming and horror words. And my mother kept coughing. Like she couldn't stop. My father didn't hear her through his hollering. He lifted a chair up and down, pounding the floor. Finally there was an empty space and silence. Except for my mother's coughs and sobs. Her face and hands were red and wet like unfrozen strawberries. I asked if she might be catching a cold because of her cough. She stained a dishcloth with her tears, then whispered, "Sometimes I choke on my thoughts."

But you can't really choke on thoughts. So what did my mother mean?

My new bed has a matching chest of drawers and a dresser with a huge mirror that attaches with rods and clips and screws. There was a lot of swearing when my parents put that mirror up. It shakes back and forth if you run around, and then the room trembles and goes all scribble-scrabble. I don't like that mirror. Most of the dresser drawers are empty because I have nothing to put in them. That drawer space gives the snakes all the room they need to keep on multiplying. But my parents say the bedroom set will be mine forever, even when I get married. So someday I'll fill the drawers. Then the snakes will have to leave. With sheets and towels and sweaters crammed in to suffocate them.

My mother places two figurines of the Blessed Virgin Mary on the dresser. Each is standing on a snake, barefoot. The real Virgin Mary pulverizes snakes by stepping on them cuz God has bestowed upon her immaculate feet that are entirely venom-proof. If regular people touch Satan's snakes, we're bitten, and poison rushes through our veins and kills us dead. Body and soul. But these two Marys are imposters. They smile too hard and are wearing blush and eye makeup. The real BVM would never do that. Neither of these Marys could kill a snake. I can tell. That's why, every night, the snakes slither out from under their feet and breed in the dresser drawers and under my bed.

They hiss when my parents shout, and then Satan starts in with his stories. Noah used to be brave and strong, saving God's two-by-two little stuffed creatures in matching colors, one held by me, the other by my mother, as they marched into his big ark—a shoebox on an old blue towel. Satan sneers that Noah's real life was nothing like how my mother and I play it. He knows because he was there. An angry and mean God-the-Father told Noah He would command the rain to drown the whole world. And then everything would be bloated and drifting and dead, with a horrible blue smell. Noah was so terrified that he might not build a boat in time to save the animals that he didn't sleep for over one hundred days and one hundred nights.

As I cling to my covers and Satan makes my mother shriek at my father that he'd drive a saint insane, Satan hisses to me that Noah did go insane, his mind drowning in sleeplessness and all that pressure from God-the-Father. There's proof of Noah's madness in our midst today. Cuz after Noah pushed and prodded animals like lions and sheep and cats and zebras and dogs all on board—he then decided to save a lot of annoying insects, like mosquitoes and Japanese beetles—the scourge of my mother's few roses, which she planted, somewhat unsuccessfully, to disguise our ugly cement garage.

So who knows how many other really nice animals there were, gentle and loving with fur in rainbow colors, that Noah left behind while catching wasps in his butterfly net? Like my Uncle Johnny, maybe Noah had gone a little mental. All because of God-the-Father, know what I mean?

I try to stop Satan by talking about Jesus who brought light into the world. Satan wants only dark like night and shadows and thick black illnesses. Jesus made blind people see. He cured leopards. Even though I don't know what was wrong with them. He turned water into wine. That's a miracle a lot of my relatives talk about whenever they have to go to the liquor store. They're always hoping it will happen to them.

But even Jesus can't protect me from these nightmare stories. Satan fills my room with God-the-Father's plagues and pestilences. Plagues are the worst because I know just how true they are, not only from the Bible, but from my parents. The snakes smell my fear and wriggle up my bedposts. My own father's mother died of the plague of tuberculosis when he was only eight years old. Right here in Cambridge. In the same city where we live. When my father was a baby, his mother was already so sick that she didn't have the strength to hold him. He wasn't ever allowed to cuddle up to her in bed the way I do with my parents on Saturday mornings when it's okay for me to bring my germs into their bed cuz my mother washes the sheets immediately once we all get up.

My little-boy-father never saw his mother outside of her bed. Her bedroom door was always shut, and once a day his father opened it so my father could go in and be with her. The room had an odd smell, probably because they never changed the sheets, but my father thought it was the smell of Death. He couldn't touch his mother since she was contagious, and she'd try to smile but then would start coughing up blood and he had to leave. My mother says that everything was totally on the q.t. back then about the TB plague. That people thought less of you if someone in your family had it. Cuz it comes from being unclean. And low class. And it's a curse from God-the-Father. A heavy, runny, sinister illness. So we can't—even now—mention it. Only Satan can.

My father doesn't ever say a word about his mother. She and her TB are huge family secrets. Satan murmurs—and the snakes rattle their tongues on my pillows—that his own presence in my room better be on the q.t. too. Who'll believe me if I tell? I'll be a mental case, like Uncle Johnny. I try to hide from Satan by sliding to the bottom of my endless bed, where the sheets are cool at first. But when I'm deep in my covers, Satan's sticky voice thunders across my room, forcing me to think about other mothers dying. Then I feel like Noah. Like I'll never sleep again. Knowing that my very own mother could die, just like my father's mother.

And my mother really did almost die. Satan reminds me night after night of something I'm definitely not supposed to know. God sent the plague of scarlet fever to my poor mother when she was only eight years old. Eight must be a terrible age. Satan breathes hotly through my covers that scarlet fever was a particularly cruel plague because it mostly affected innocent children. My poor little-girl-mother, sick with scarlet fever, had to stay in the hospital for two months and couldn't see her own mother or anyone in her family—that's how contagious she was.

So many kids were dying of scarlet fever that two girls were put into each hospital bed. My little-girl-mother remembers different bedmates. Why do I know this? I think Satan made Nana tell me.

My mother's bedmates always seemed older than she was and comforted her in the evenings when she would cry and cry because she missed her mother, and the older girl would stroke her hair, saying she'd get better and go home soon. That would help my mother fall asleep. But when she woke up in the morning and started to talk to her bedmate or tried to wake her up, the girl was dead. Frozen stiff.

My mother remembers being too weak to leave the bed to get help. So she just screamed. And she screamed and screamed but nobody came for a long time cuz so many children's souls had been taken away from them by God-the-Father in the night, leaving only cold, hard bodies. And there weren't enough nurses. After my mother's bedmates kept dying every night, she began wondering why she was always the one to still be alive.

A nurse read her psalms, saying she was special and chosen by God to live. "Though a thousand fall at your side, and ten thousand at your right side; near you it shall not come." She didn't feel chosen. Kind of like Noah.

Like my father's mother dying for eight years in her bed, my mother's waking up when she was eight years old with a different dead girl morning after morning is another major family secret. I once asked Nana how it was to live those months without my little-girl-mother in a time of famine and plagues and pestilence and so many deaths. But she said we should talk about something more pleasant or play cards or fill two empty bottles with water and hide them in the cupboard to see if they'd turn into wine in time for my cousin's wedding. We did. They didn't.

I don't think Satan has the power to kill me with a plague, but he tries. I have a stomach ache most of the time, and we go to Dr. Whalen's a lot. He gives all kids the same medicine. Chocolate water with ground-up aspirins in it. That medicine makes me vomit and then my stomach hurts more. Dr. Whalen says we need to have faith and give it time to work. But we already have twelve bottles in our pantry. As he's writing the prescription, my mother asks if he's giving me something different this time, and he nods his balding head. Even though when we get it filled, it's always more chocolate aspirin.

I'm safer from Satan and the snakes if I stay under the covers at the bottom of my bed. But sometimes it gets so hot I creep back up, and the air feels wonderful, like I just ate an orange Popsicle, and the pillows are so soft and clean that I forget about Satan and plagues and dead mothers and fall asleep. Those nights I wake up shouting, my hands tangled in my long hair up to my wrists, my head rolling from side to side. My parents rush in and put on the light. "It's Satan again," I whisper to my mother cuz we all know what my father thinks about my night fears. "His snakes crawled into my hair. I have to pull them out before they get to my neck and strangle me."

"Did you hear her?" my mother mutters with her teeth clenched to my father.

"Satan, Schmatan. She's just pulling her own hair."

This happens almost every night if I don't sleep hidden way under, deep in the hot covers.

"Get a wet facecloth to cool her down," my mother sighs. My father's expression is a shard of glass. My mother strokes my head. "Be still, Bridget, so I can untangle you."

She finally loosens my sweaty hands and pulls out a tissue from her pink bathrobe that gives me the creeps because it has rose bugs printed all over it. Why would anyone, especially my mother—who stops whatever she's doing and searches the apartment, armed with a wet dishcloth and a fly swatter, if even a single mosquito gets in, cursing Noah the whole time—buy a bathrobe covered in bugs? Little pink, misshapen bodies with green ugly feet. I guess they're aphids cuz they're way too small to be Japanese beetles. But still, that robe must have been on a really good sale.

"C'mon, Bridget. Blow your nose now." I'm still lying down, so half the snots slide into my throat.

My father enters with a dripping washcloth. Glaring at him and then me, my mother shakes her head. "Can't you at least wring it out?"

His sigh is so loud. She won't complain again. He bangs a cup down.

The cloth rubs against my face and up into my hair. It wets the pillow. Still feels cool. I sip lukewarm water. Quick kisses, soft murmurs, "Back to sleep now, Bridget." As if nothing's wrong. "Night-night." Out the door.

I usually do get back to sleep. But only if I don't pay attention to the snakes, daring me to get out of bed and step on one of them. Or to touch the shadow on my bedroom door. My mother says it comes from the telephone pole outside my window. But I know that shadow is the arm of the Devil. Showing the snakes which way to slither toward me. They'd all attack me if I got up.

One night when I can't fall back to sleep because the snakes are so noisy, I call to my mother from my bed. She sits by me, but is a little irritated. "Where do these snakes actually come from, Bridget?" She glances around the room, hinting she doesn't see any.

"Escape from the statues. Listen hard—rattling now in the drawers and under my bed." I don't know if she hears them or not. But she gasps and whisks the statues off my dresser. "I'll wrap them tightly in a plastic bag and hide them in the bottom of a cupboard in the pantry."

The next morning she rushes in to ask if Satan and the snakes are gone and if I'm better. When I tell her that they all came back, she looks so sad.

Really. What did she expect? I mean, it's Satan. If he found me all the way from hell, he's certainly going to find me from the pantry. And even though it's daytime, the snakes slide out of the dresser, leaving slimy marks on the floor. They hiss that they're angry I told my mother where they come from. They want everything on the q.t. too.

Even though it's daytime, Satan laughs out loud.

3. The Holy in the Holy Water

Satan is now swirling through our apartment like the cold blue ice in my father's eyes. Daddy looks at me and shakes his head. My mother understands, I think. Daddy doesn't want to. The three of us have to keep it on the q.t. He pounds his fist on the table. No one can ever be told that Satan is in living in my bedroom. Or that I scream at night. Or how I pull my hair in my sleep to get the snakes out. I've created a terrible new family secret. In a family that has enough already. My father won't even look at me.

The two of them argue more than ever once I'm in bed. A dark ooze smears over my walls and curtains and ceiling. It turns into locusts that surge madly around me until I squirm far into my covers. I'd rather suffocate than be hit in the face by one of those creatures.

Even with all those locusts, I can still hear my parents' voices like thin crushed glass scraped against hard tiles on kitchen walls. "There is no Satan," my father insists. "She's not having nightmares about snakes from hell. She just wakes herself up because, like some kind of nutcase, she pulls her own hair."

"What's your point?" my mother shouts.

"That by taking a perfectly normal fear of the dark so seriously, you've let her make it worse and

28

worse." When he repeats words, the rooms tremble. Even the locusts stop.

"Well, what should we do?" My mother's crying again. Can she sense the locusts, even though I've never mentioned them.

"Stop indulging the child!" he yells. "You seem to have no sense how crazy she sounds!" The words splash through his spitty voice. He gets that way when he's mad.

Satan lifts up my covers and grins at me, his eyes smoldering bright red.

"Get out of here!" I shriek. "You can't look inside. It's supposed to be safe under the covers!" Satan drops my bed linens but commands locusts to dive at me until I'm rolled in a tight ball.

After months of fighting, nightlights of varying degrees of brightness, and absolutely no let up from Satan, my parents decide to break the family secret rule and ask Dr. Whalen for help. My father gets the last appointment on a Friday so we won't meet people. Cuz everyone goes to Dr. Whalen. He ushers us into the examining room and talks with my parents for a few minutes about my nightmares.

No one asks me anything. So I don't say a word. And Dr. Whalen never finds out about Satan. Or his bedtime stories. Or the snakes. Or even that I pull my hair when I'm trying to yank them out so they can't strangle me. Shouldn't someone explain to Dr. Whalen that if the snakes kill me, they'll take me, dead, to Satan and his filthy home in hell the way Pluto took Persephone in my *Great Stories from the Greeks and Romans* book? Except my mother isn't Demeter. So she won't be able to find me, and I'll burn for all eternity.

If they told Dr. Whalen all this, he'd realize that I'm not having nightmares. He'd understand that it's all real, know what I mean?

Dr. Whalen smiles at me and tousles my head. Then he examines my eyes and ears and feels my tummy. Finally he brings us to his office and we all sit down. "Nightmares like Bridget's are almost always caused by anxiety."

My parents jump out of their seats. My father points his finger across Dr. Whalen's desk, right at his face. If he had a bow and arrow, I know he'd shoot Dr. Whalen then and there. Right in his eye, which would now be hanging out of his head, all gooey and broken. "Don't be ridiculous! What does a child her age have to be anxious about?" my father yells. Dr. Whalen pauses. He stares at each of my parents with both of his eyes. I can hear the faint hum of locusts. The moan of frogs. "I don't rightly know," he says. Sounding like he does.

My father picks up on Dr. Whalen's tone, and his Irish-white skin becomes deep red. He pushes us out of that office, shouting over his shoulder, "No doubt she's suffering from nothing at all, but now you've gone and made it worse." My father's almost got us out the door when he turns back. "If it weren't so close to dinnertime, I'd stay and give you a piece of my mind. We pay you to cure problems, not cause them." My father likes to eat at exactly 5:30 every night. And he hates discussions of "anxiety" or mental issues cuz of Uncle Johnny and his anxiety about how noisy the war was.

I guess once you break the family secret rule, even a little, it's easier to do it again. Because my mother brings me to one of our St. Michael's parish priests. 'Course it's on the q.t. We can't exactly tell my father. I'm now responsible for way too many family secrets.

We walk around the dark living room of the priest house where divine advice is given until Father Duffy comes in. He's fat and smokes constantly, and even though I don't go to school yet,

I know everyone calls him Puffy Duffy. My mother doesn't know that 'cause it's a secret for kids—totally on the q.t. for adults. Father Duffy tells us to sit down. I do. My mother paces around him as she explains my screaming and hair-pulling, though there's no mention of Satan or the snakes.

He lights a cigarette and seems to be only vaguely paying attention to her. He sits on the couch next to me. Through the odor of tobacco, he smells like he needs a bath. He smiles and pats my head with his puffy hand. Finally he makes my mother sit in one of the chairs.

"Nightmares like Bridget's are almost always caused by guilt."

My mother stands up, grabs me, and glares at him. "Bridget's as good as gold and has nothing to be guilty about." Then she pulls me out of the priests' living room faster than my father got us out of the doctor's office. I don't think she likes Father Duffy anyway cuz her family always complains how the Catholic Church was hijacked in America by the Irish. Most of my Italian relations wouldn't set foot inside an Irish church, let alone a priest house. Except for a wedding or a funeral.

One rainy summer morning, after my father leaves for work, my mother tells me something amazing. "I have a solution to your nightmares, and Satan and the snakes, Bridget, but it has to be on the q.t. from your father," she says softly. As if he could hear her all the way from his job.

"Will you promise to do whatever I ask?" I nod.

"Today we're enlisting support from your guardian angel and all three members of the Holy Trinity. And they'll help me drive Satan and his snakes out of your bedroom. Starting tonight. Our first stop is the Catholic store." I hold my mother's hand very tightly as we walk to our bus stop.

At the Catholic store my mother speaks forcefully. "One font, small enough to hang in a doorway, with an angel on it. And it must be a happy-looking child angel. We can't have any religious drama." I want to warn her that a child angel might not frighten Satan but don't dare.

"After we get home, Bridey, and once we've washed our hands, we'll unwrap your guardian angel, wash her, and have lunch. And then we'll take a clean bottle to church to get some holy water."

We always have to wash our hands when we come in from the outside because there are germs everywhere. Especially outside. They're invisible. So you don't know if they've attached themselves to you. But they can kill. Germs are microscopic, blood-sucking centipedes. They're the cause of every single plague, and since my mother survived one, she's a real expert. Sometimes germs stealthily enter your body right through your skin, and you have no control over these vampire organisms whose sole aim is to make you sick by dividing and multiplying under your skin and getting into your blood and drinking it until you have none left. And then you die. Unless God determines, in His infinite wisdom, to spare you.

Swallowing germs is also dangerous because then they have direct access to your stomach. Once inside, they eat your food as well as drink your blood, so you get weak faster. But most of the time, if you consume germs through your mouth, it's your own fault cuz you didn't take care to wash every single one of them off your hands. And God helps those who help themselves, so if you're responsible for letting germs get inside your own body, you can hardly expect Him (or my mother) to be sympathetic. Especially, you know, since He's not all that sympathetic anyway.

You get billions more germs on you when you take the bus cuz you touch places where other people—particularly non-Catholics who don't know that "cleanliness is next to Godliness" and who therefore don't wash their hands all the time—have been holding on. And since it's the summer, their hands are probably sweaty, which provides the ideal environment for spreading germs. Everyone knows that germs love it when the bus handles become warm and moist because they multiply and spread from one person to another, gaining strength all the time. So when we get home, I'm sure we'll wash our hands twice. Once for the outside. And once for the bus. Then we'll wash them again before lunch cuz, even in your own house, regardless of how clean you are, microbes are lurking and eager to sneak inside you on your food. God-the-Father is still sending out His plagues and pestilences. But no one writes about them anymore because the world is becoming less religious.

As my mother washes my guardian angel in a pan of hot, soapy water, she explains that the angel is standing on a holy water font. Holy water, which we've never had in our house before, is going to be our big weapon against Satan. "You and I will hang the font on the door frame right outside your bedroom to guard you, Bridget, and we'll refill it every few days so it's never dry." I nod my head. This isn't a time to interrupt, know what I mean?

"You'll dip your finger in and bless yourself with the holy water every night, in the name of the whole Trinity—the Father, the Son, and the Holy Ghost. And I'll do the same." I'm pretty surprised my mother thinks holy water is the solution, but I can feel my stomach start to loosen already. "We won't ask Daddy to bless himself, at least at first, okay?" I smile. I'll do whatever my mother wants. "Even though your dad used to be an altar boy and was so religious, you know how he sometimes says that stuff like holy water and relics are a lot of BS. So until he notices you aren't waking up in the middle of the night anymore, it'll just be our little secret." 'Course I agree.

But I'm confused. My mother is always repulsed by the holy water in the fonts at church with all its stagnant finger germs. "Don't dip!" she whispers loudly when we go in. She's always reminding me that the rules about covering your mouth when you sneeze or cough are all well and good for keeping the air clean, but they make people's hands so infected that even the slightest contact can be dangerous. And germs slip off someone's fingers much more quickly if they get wet, which is why holy water is so unsanitary. Often one of the priests, who all seem pretty clueless about disease contraction, is standing just inside the church to greet people when they come in. And then we have to do a fake dunking where we put our fingers into the font, but we don't actually touch the water. We make the sign of the cross with dry fingers and remain physically clean. Even if our souls are slightly less purified.

"Then, once you get into bed," my mother continues, "I'll get more holy water and sprinkle you, to bless you. And the bed. And under the bed. And the floor. And the whole room." We won't have to worry about germs in my holy water because it'll be a private font for only my mother and me. And I'm sure we'll wash our hands before we dip. "And then everything will be safe. Between the holy water and my invocation of the Trinity, the Devil and the snakes will be driven away." I've never seen anyone bless a room before except Bishop O'Brien, and that was in St. Michael's Church. I didn't even realize a regular person like my mother could do such holy things.

When we get to the church, my mother opens one of the heavy oak doors, and a faint scent of incense and holy dustiness envelops us. I breathe in deeply, knowing I'm smelling God. The church's holy water container is conveniently located in a small, separate room in the back so that parishioners can get as much holy water as they need without disturbing whatever might be happening in the actual church. Like a Mass or a wedding or a funeral. I know this because they frequently announce it after Mass. But today nothing is going on.

The holy water urn looks like the giant coffee dispenser Lucy's parents have for parties. When they aren't using it, her mother leaves it open and lying sideways on a shelf in their pantry so it can air out and won't get moldy. But Lucy and I know that her cat likes to sleep in it. If I were a grown-up, I'd never want to have coffee at Lucy's house. The holy water urn is about three feet high with one of those on/off levers that lets the holy water come out of a small faucet. It sits on a tall stand that comes up to my shoulders. My mother removes a clean glass chocolate-aspirin medicine bottle from her purse. It's wrapped in one of Daddy's large, white handkerchiefs. Carefully twisting off the bottle cap, she says that I can hold the bottle if I promise that I'll never in a million years drop it. My hands sweat as I place the bottle under the spout. My mother pushes the little lever.

Nothing happens. She makes a face and tries again. Not a drop. She lightly taps the urn, putting her good ear close to it. The one that the doctor didn't have to cut the eardrum out of to get rid of the germy pus of scarlet fever that would have gone to my little-girl-mother's brain and killed her. Then she starts hitting the urn all over. Eventually my mother is making quite a racket and mutters what I think is a swear word or two.

"Never mind, Bridget, don't you worry. We're getting whatever holy water we can squeeze out of this thing," she says, sounding kind of angry. "We haven't spent the whole day preparing only to go home without anything." Her voice scares me. What if we do have to go home without any holy water? Satan will know. And the stories he'll have tonight will be unbearable.

Suddenly my mother grabs the urn, lifts it off its stand, and drops it to the floor. It makes a loud bang and doesn't balance well. "Hold onto it, Bridey. We have to do this fast before anyone comes in. I'm taking the top off to see how much water we're dealing with." We're being pretty irreverent for church behavior. Even if my mother doesn't like the Irish priests. I decide, despite the germs, to sit on the floor so I can wrap my arms and legs around the urn. She doesn't even notice. The stone floor feels cold and gritty. My mother's face is purple as she strains to get the cover off. Finally it flies up in the air and crashes down on the floor. We sure are lucky we're alone.

My mother peers into the open urn. "Oh for Christsake!" she cries out and makes a gagging sound, rushing to the church door.

"What's in there, Mommy?" I ask.

She's rummaging through her purse. "I have to get a peppermint." This is a bad sign. My mother always has to suck on a peppermint when her stomach feels sick.

Like an idiot, I'm still sitting on the floor so I can't even see into the urn. I get up slowly, careful that I don't let it tip. But if there's a snake in there, I'm just going to drop that urn and run. Even if the parish bulletin next week broadcasts that there's been a mysterious desecration of the holy water. I don't care. If Satan has invaded the urn, we've all been abandoned by God anyway, know what I mean? I stand up and breathe in the choky church air and force myself to look.

Oh! We're saved! I can hear the angels singing in my head. Heavenly hosts of them fly around me. The realization that few people are as blessed as we have just become overwhelms me. My mother doesn't want to gawk. I can't help it. Because there, at the bottom of the urn, in about an inch of water, is what must be, as I stare at it, The Holy itself.

The urn is usually closed so tightly because only priests who are consecrated to God forever are allowed to gaze upon The Holy. But we're blameless cuz we only came to get holy water. That God would let us see The Holy is surely a sign it was ordained by Him for us to realize how powerfully concentrated this water is. Water that we're going to bring home to my sacred font. Water that's going to be strong enough to fight Satan. The Holy just floats there. About four inches long. Green and loosely ruffled. So delicate is The Holy that it would melt or break if you tried to pull it out. 'Course, I never would. Not with my unblessed, germy, human hands. It's such a bright green. Maybe my father and the priests are right that God is Irish, not Italian.

My mother turns around slowly. She's really upset. "How can I bring that into our house, even after all I promised you?" She must think it's very wrong to have looked directly into The Holy.

"It's okay, Mom," I whisper. "I've seen it and I know God isn't angry. We don't have to tell anyone." More secrets. But it seems impossible to avoid them.

"Bridget," my mother says. I can hear the peppermint in her mouth. "You must never put your fingers to your lips or, God forbid, in your mouth after you've touched that water." Her teeth are clenched, and she still looks kind of sick.

As I gently rock the urn, I watch The Holy glide weightlessly back and forth and know that it must make the last little waves of holy water in the urn so blessed that putting any of it in my mouth would be like taking Communion. And I haven't received my First Communion yet. So that would be a sin. I smile at my mother and assure her that even after my First Communion, I'll never put a trace of holy water in my mouth.

"All right," she shudders and comes over with the bottle. "You tip the urn toward the spout, and I'll push the lever to get some water."

It's hard to orchestrate it all, but we do it. After we put everything back in place and walk outside, my mother holds the bottle up to the bright sunlight. She's checking that no Holy got in. I know it. She realizes how special it is too. She knows that by swishing the small amount of water in the urn around all that Holy, we've ended up with very potent and powerful holy water.

"Thank God," she says.

Thank God, indeed, I think.

We wash up quickly when we get home. My mother hammers a nail into my doorframe, and together we hang the guardian angel font up through a hole in her back. "If you want," she says, "I'll let you help me pour in the first batch of holy water." We don't spill a drop. Then we practice blessing ourselves and my bedroom. It feels so good, you know what I mean?

After dinner, my mother gives me a Golden Book on the Blessed Virgin that she must have also bought in the Catholic store. It has lovely pictures of Mary and Joseph and Jesus. The Holy Family.

"Is this a new book?" my father asks, taking it from me and checking the price. Then he leafs through it.

"Yes," I nod, wanting to tell him everything about the font and the holy water and The Holy, but I don't say anything because, for the moment, it definitely has to be on the q.t.

He hands the book back to me and smiles. "It's good for a girl to have books on the Blessed Mother. You can learn a lot about meekness and mildness. Things that you won't learn otherwise in this house."

If he's referring to my mother, I think this must be one of the kinds of belittling comments she doesn't like. I know that she did rip one of his shirts right off his back last week. And they're still getting over that fight. But she also gives in to him almost all of the time. About our food. When we can go out. What we can do. And the big one—how much we can spend on anything. And she does so much work in the house. And I help her. I'd like to see him fix the tenants' leaky toilets and dripping faucets. He can't even make a plumb line as well as I can, though I'm still a little afraid on the big ladder. Plus I don't want her to be meek and mild. I want a mother who's able to fight Satan for my soul. And that's just what she's doing.

Finally it's night and we can try it all out. When my mother gets into her nightclothes and I climb into bed, she has to dip her finger into the guardian angel font seven times to get enough water to sanctify each part of my room. She sprinkles holy water all over the place. Under my bed. On my covers. In the drawers. Even in my two closets. I feel so safe that I build up the courage to ask her why she ever bought a bathrobe with rose bugs on it. Especially since she loves roses so much. And hates bugs.

"Bridey, honey, they're rose buds, not rose bugs!" She laughs and looks a little concerned, all in the same instant. "Do we need to clean out your ears? Can you imagine me wearing something with bugs on it? Especially to bed!" She hugs me again and then goes off to tell my father about "the funniest misunderstanding." Though I know she's not going to mention the holy water.

She probably won't ever tell him. Still, it's wonderful to have it. And to have a mother like her. I just wish it all didn't have to be a secret. Not to mention the bathrobe. I'm so relieved but also feel kind of odd about it in a way I can't explain. Why hadn't I known? Why did those buds seem so convincingly to be bugs?

But then I just stop and think about the day. I have my own holy water font. I helped my mother put it up. We poured the first tiny stream of my very holy holy water into it. My mother's not wearing rose bugs. She can bless rooms and she sprinkled holy droplets everywhere in mine. We were divinely chosen to actually see The Holy. How many people can say that? Satan has got one big battle on his hands.

4. At the Kitchen Window I: Window Washing

The best view from our second-floor apartment is through the kitchen window. You can almost see the firehouse two blocks away. When anything's happening outside, that's the window we all run to.

My mother throws stale bread out to the birds from that window. I watch them land so quickly, as if they'd been on the lookout for us. The sparrows and the pigeons get there first. They try to pick out the center. But the greedy, cawing crows swoop in and fly off with whole pieces that nearly cover their heads. I always root for the sparrows, even though they only ever get a few crumbs.

While my mother keeps our house extremely clean, she isn't all that fussy about windows, except that kitchen one. And it's not cuz of germs. "If we're going to look out, we might as well be able to see," she says, usually after I've marked the window with a nose or fingerprint.

So, about twice a month, except in the dead of winter, I'm summoned. And my mother and I engage in the intricate process of window washing. She has her spray bottle with an ammonia-and-water potion she makes herself and various folded cloths cut from my father's old flannel pajamas. And she doesn't just clean the inside or the bottom half of the window, as one might expect. She's thorough. My mother washes every part of that window.

Spray. Ammonia. Eye sting. Nose tingle. Wipe vigorously with Dad's old pajama shirt. Watch out for unremoved buttons. Watch out for streaks. Spray. Sting. Tingle. Wipe. Repeat. Spray. Sting. Tingle. Wipe. Repeat. Spray. Sting. Tingle. Wipe. Repeat. Know what I mean?

Washing windows is a tricky business. It isn't just about getting the glass clean but about moving the windows themselves. One careless action and everything could go wrong. The inside windows are old. They work on a rope system and have to be moved up and down carefully cuz the ropes are fraying and could snap. And then the window would come crashing down, possibly shattering the glass. Or the finger of the person trying to stop its fall. Heads could roll if you pushed a window up too fast and broke its rope.

The outside storm windows are equally dangerous. They're so heavy. You have to heave them up, high and fast, to lock them into position. You can't let go until you hear a faint click. Cuz if you don't hold on carefully, they'd shoot down, fast as the wind, and guillotine your arm off.

Once the insides of the four windows are washed, it's time for the outsides. My mother takes a deep breath and slowly lifts the old bottom window, quickly raises the storm, then bends over backward and shimmies herself under the windows and out into the air until she can angle her torso back up and sit on the windowsill and lower a window. Her legs are still inside the kitchen, and one of my jobs is to hold them tightly while the rest of her body is outside.

When she's ready, my mother sticks her right hand in and shakes it, her fingers opening and closing. In an instant I must hand her the ammonia-

42

water bottle and a clean cloth. We're not allowed to talk during this phase of window washing because it's too risky.

Invariably there's some bird poop inconveniently deposited in a difficult-to-reach corner of the window. Then my mother has to sit back farther than she usually would, contort her arm to reach it, spray it, and rub it off. As the bird poop streaks white all over the window, my mother breaks her vow of silence to curse the birds. "Filthy things! I'll never feed you damn birds again."

'Course I know she will, but I'm not to respond. My job is to hold her legs. If I let go of her even for an instant, she could plunge two stories down and be impaled on my metal swing set below and stung by the hornets that live there.

For years we paint that swing set every spring— red, green, and yellow—matching the original colors. My mother taught me how to sand off the rust before painting—first with a rough piece of sandpaper and then with a fine one to make the metal nice and smooth. And she, with her face covered in cheesecloth, sprays Raid into the hornets' nest inside the top bar of the swing set and then runs like the devil back into the house. From the kitchen window we watch the hornets buzz out, some dazed and dying, others zipping away. After it looks like they've all vacated, my mother puts steel wool into what we hope is their ex-nest. But no matter what we do, the rust comes back and so do the hornets. Still, I love the swing set and the fact that when my parents and Pa Joe first put it up for me and cemented it into the ground, they wrote my name in the wet cement. BRIDEY AGE 5 holds down the front right pole.

Sometimes I get tired holding my mother's legs, but not as tired as her back and arms get, as she often reminds me. She's the one spraying and wiping and maneuvering the windows up and down to get the four outside sides clean. Altogether eight sides. A lot of washing for just one window. But when we finish, the window is almost invisible. I'm sure most people don't have a window like that.

Maybe that's why, one day, I'm able to see farther than I ever have. Because that window is so clean. The sky is cloudless and the birds are chirping as well as pooping when the moment comes. I see, in an instant, that I could push my mother out of the window.

Not that I would. Or that I would ever want to. Not in the least. Only that I realize what I had not until that moment known, and I don't want to know it, and I pray that the recognition will vanish from my thoughts, but it won't. I could kill my mother.

And not only do I know I could, but I see that my mother must know and trust me not to. Do I want such trust placed in me? Do I want that much responsibility?

And does my mother think about the implications of the position I am in? Does she understand or did she even imagine that, at some point, I would know, I would realize, in a single moment, that I had the option, the free will, to do just the thing that I was trusted not to do?

I am shattered.

5. Bishop O'Brien's *Child's Guide To Avoiding Temptation* & The Perils of Sylvia Destephano

"Bridg-et! You are whipping Christ, right before He is to carry the cross! Can't you see the blood oozing from the wounds you're inflicting on His back?"

No! Not again! I can't believe how often I've been going back and forth to Calvary this year—and all without my own volition and usually while I'm eating tuna fish sandwiches during lunch at school, and completely on the q.t., even from myself.

The horror of the third grade is the discovery that—as Sister Louise has explained—we can travel through time and hurt people from the past and sometimes the present and, most especially, Jesus on Calvary. Without knowing we're doing it.

"Do you realize that children in Africa will be more hungry today than they were yesterday? All because of you, Bridget!" Sister Louise hollers.

"Yes," I lie. I knew that being eight years old would be terrible after what happened to my parents at that age—my mother almost dying of scarlet fever and my father's mother dying of TB. Now I'm time-traveling to hurt Jesus and African children. I hate being eight.

Our class is almost finished having lunch. At our desks. Without having washed our hands. And after three people have already thrown up cuz the room is so hot. The heat is on, banging through the radiators, even though we're having a very long, very warm Indian summer. I slowly inch my tuna fish sandwich up the waxed paper my mother wrapped it in, careful not to touch the bread with my sweaty fingers. Sister Louise is standing over me with an ashen white face. I haven't been in the third grade long enough yet to learn if it's worse when Sister Louise turns white or red. The tuna fish is oozing out of the bread and onto the waxed paper, which is getting soggy. I lick the ooze and take another small bite. With nuns, the older kids have told us, it's always one way or the other—red or white—and you have to find out fast.

Sister Louise was even more than usually annoyed with me this morning when I finished my subtraction test so quickly.

"Come on, children! Move along! Exercise those God-given arithmetic abilities!" she goaded us into hurrying and making a mistake. I actually possess significant God-given subtraction skills, which I thought Sister would approve of when I brought my finished test up to her desk in less than ten minutes. But she seemed angry that I got all the problems right.

"You might be good at subtraction, Bridget, but that's hardly going to garner God's love if you don't renounce your vanity about your math skills." She's a difficult person to please.

Suddenly Sister grabs the sandwich out of my hands and rips the paper off it, her fingers spreading her germs all over the bread. Then she gives it back to me to infect with my own hands.

"Will you kindly hurry up?" she yells, in an unkindly tone. "For someone who does her math and reading faster than she should, I can't understand how you're the slowest eater in the class, probably in the whole school." As she turns to leave, she flashes back around, shaking her finger at me. "I'll see you, girl, after school."

Definitely white.

Everyone clears out of the classroom faster than usual cuz the temperature has become unbearable. And two more kids vomited. I wait, sitting at my desk, stuck to the chair, for Sister Louise to return from walking the rest of the class to the street corner. With my book bag packed, I put on the sweater my mother makes me wear back and forth to school, regardless of the temperature. But almost instantly I realize the sweater's a mistake. My cheeks start to burn with the heat and my stomach gets queasy. Sister's taking so long. I pull my arms out of the sweater, holding tightly to each cuff, like my mother has taught me, so I won't turn a sleeve inside out, and I'm just getting it over my head when Sister Louise charges in.

"Bridget, pay attention!"

I push my head back through the sweater. The rest of it dangles idiotically around my neck. She stands over me.

"I have a surprise for you."

Why don't those words sound good, like when my mother says them? I notice a book in her hand.

"Well," she clears her throat, "you can think of it as more of a small penance," and she flashes me that really unpleasant smirk she gets right before throwing an eraser across the classroom at one of the boys. She does have an excellent aim.

"I've talked with Sister Superior, and we've decided to give you a copy of Bishop O'Brien's *Child's Guide to Avoiding Temptation and Staying on the Path to God*, even though we normally give this book only to older children. But Sister knows you're such a good reader, and with what I've told her about you...." She stops and pushes the book at me.

It opens to the dedication page. "This book is written in commemoration of my visit to Rome, Vatican II, 3rd session." And there's a scribbly signature, which I think says "Bishop O'Brien."

I didn't realize he'd been abroad. Or that they talk about children in the Vatican Councils. I feel quite impressed at the bishop for writing a book for children about his travels, even though I can't actually find his name on the book anywhere. I plan to travel a lot when I grow up, though probably never to a Vatican Council. Not with my record on the children in Africa. I start to flip the pages, looking for pictures of Rome or any interesting tourist routes, when Sister squeezes the book shut.

"So, Sister Superior and I want you to pay particular attention to the sections on pride. They might be of more help to you than your books of religious stories."

I love my Bible stories and my Greek and Roman myth books. Whenever there's a question in class about Daniel or Isaac, or Zeus, or the Annunciation or Mary Magdalene or any of the Virgin Martyrs, whom I am starting to collect Holy Cards of, I'm always ready to tell everyone all about them. My friends Lucy and Agnes, and sometimes Anne, even though she isn't Catholic, and I spend many happy afternoons acting out what we find to be the most exciting Saint stories, which are usually those involving a fallen woman. Or a virgin who refused to fall. Either type is likely to be stoned to death, but it's the falling, not the stoning, that interests us. We talk about what it might be like to become "fallen"? There always seems to be a man who causes it, usually a pagan general or a muscular centurion carrying a spear or a sword. Lucy and Agnes and I decide falling must have something to do with what all our mothers call "the down there."

Moving away from my desk, Sister Louise glares at me with cold eyes. "Remember, Bridget, your intelligence could prove to be just as much a curse as a blessing." And with that, I'm dismissed.

I long to be good and have my parents and God love me. I don't want to be turned into a pillar of salt. Or be given running sores. Or have Roman centurions or rampaging pagans do unspeakable things to my body parts, with their spears or anything else, like what they did to Virgin Martyrs. And I can't have Satan and his snakes return to my bedroom. So I start reading Bishop O'Brien's book every night before I go to sleep, even though it isn't about his travels at all.

It's a scary book, mostly about my worst fears of the Devil haunting and possessing children who are such an easy prey for him. I need such courage to leave my bed and cross the floor to my holy water font. Then I can sprinkle the water everywhere and sometimes even hold up my glowing crucifix, which I'm still not sure I like.

But one night, while I'm reading the *Guide*, I'm so relieved to discover that my soul is safe. I'm not going to be tempted into the sin of pride by the Devil or anything else cuz he isn't after me anymore. Every part of my body and soul relaxes. What I do learn is that the Devil has taken possession of the girl who sits next to me in school, Sylvia DeStephano. The only frightening part is that God expects me to save her. And on the q.t.

Sylvia DeStephano looks like Shirley Temple, with her big brown eyes, plump cheeks, large teeth, and ringletty hair. "My mother sets my hair in rollers every night before I go to sleep," Sylvia informed Lucy and me one afternoon as we're leaving school. Lucy and I were both glad that Sylvia has to suffer to have such glossy and bouncy hair. Lucy's frizzy red hair is always pulled back in a ponytail, and mine is in two tight braids sticking out from either side of my head. What we were all unaware of then was that Sylvia's hair was one of many signs of the dubious state of her soul.

Bishop O'Brien writes: *Beware of signs of Satan, who approaches us in many disguises. All boys and girls are subject to the influence of evil spirits. Sometimes the possessed exhibit what appear to be special gifts. Do not be easily impressed by those who seem to have extraordinary powers. They may be in league with the Devil.*

As I read these words, I think immediately of Sylvia. She displays many Satanic signs. She often doesn't wear the same itchy, navy-blue wool uniform and stiff, starched, white blouse the rest of us girls have to. Special gifts. Sylvia wears secular clothes. Disguises. One of her particularly annoying outfits comes into my mind. A sailor suit in a bright-peach color. Ugly, but expensive. You can just tell.

Do not be easily impressed...

I fall asleep to the thought of Sylvia's being in league with the Devil.

The next morning, after a particularly fitful night of worrying how I'll ever be able to do God's will, while walking to school and avoiding stepping on any cracks, I vow to watch Sylvia closely for more signs, remembering Bishop O'Brien's words: *For you as children are most capable of seeing God's signs which are all around us and filled with meaning.*

I enter the classroom and there is Sylvia— sending out signs like a beacon. She's wearing pink lipstick that matches a pink chiffon dress. And she has sandals on. With no socks. There's pink nail polish on her toenails. Lipstick! Bare toes in school! With nail polish! These are definitely signs. And now I recognize what they are sign of. Vanity.

"Vanity of vanities, all is vanity." Repeat this line to yourself often—when you are spending time in front of the mirror, or even in church when you find your mind wandering. Watch that you do not spend too much time thinking of yourself or trying to get others to notice you. This is a sin that can particularly affect girls who become too concerned with clothing and adornments.

Clothing and adornments. They seem to be all that Sylvia is made of.

While I'm somewhat frightened by Sylvia's sinfulness, I can't stop thinking about her adornments. Lipstick. Clothing made of delicate fabrics in shocking colors. Nail polish. Tendrilly hair. Really, a bit like snakes. My own hair is long and usually kind of wrinkly from being in braids all day. I wonder how I'd look if I curled my hair and wore lipstick. Agnes and I are sent on an errand to Woolworth's to buy her mother a shower cap, and we find ourselves going through their new nail polish collection.

We particularly like Moulin Rouge, which you can buy individually or in a boxed set with lipstick and coordinating cheek and eye colors. Agnes shows me the tweezers and nail file set she wants to ask her mother to buy for her upcoming birthday. The collection comes in a purple, patent-leather case, and they sell matching wallets and purses of various sizes. Although we're running late, Agnes and I stop off in the girls' shoe department and discover a new line of patent-leather shoes in every color for fall, including purple.

When I come home, I look in the mirror at my heavy eyebrows and wonder if Agnes's mother might want to buy me some tweezers as well. I ask my mother if I can have purple patent-leather shoes, but she says they'd be impractical. So I march out of the room and into the bathroom, where I try to comb my heavy eyebrows into a thinner line, cuz I have no way to pluck them and no possibility of acquiring attractive new fall shoes. But when I nearly stick the pointy end of the comb into my eye, I recognize that the Devil could be tempting me, through Sylvia, to become obsessed with adornments. All is vanity.

I guiltily turn away from the mirror and begin to pray: "Dear God, why are my thoughts filled with Sylvia and brightly colored patent leather? I do not want to be vain." And then honesty overtakes me, since I am, after all, talking to God. "I mean I do not want to want to be vain."

I have a lot of luck with God during this particular fall season, and He answers me right away. "I've put vain thoughts in your mind not because you are vain, my dear child, but because I want you to think of Sylvia. To help her to realize that she is possessed by evil spirits. To vanquish them. And to save her immortal soul."

What a relief it is to discover that it's God and not the Devil who's filling my mind with nail polish, brightly colored shoes with matching purses, and tweezers.

The very next day I go over to Sylvia at recess. She is, as usual, standing in the corner of the playground alone, trying not to get dirty. "Hi, Sylvia," I say more tentatively than I intended to.

She's wearing a fancy suit that looks like it's made of tapestry and for someone with royal blood, like Mary Queen of Scots, who was martyred by having her head cut off for being a Catholic in England. I know that England isn't a pagan country. They're mostly Protestants, but even though they seem nice enough here in the greater Boston area, Protestants do sometimes kill Catholics, which is probably why Grandpa Flaherty is always going on about wanting me to stay away from them.

Disguises. Sylvia must be uncomfortably warm in her royal outfit.

"Why don't you wear a uniform all the time, and why do you get to leave school when you aren't sick?" I blurt out before I lose my courage.

Sylvia raises her well-groomed eyebrows and smiles at me the way grown-ups do when you ask them something stupid. "I am a child model for Filene's," she says, and then quickly adds, "Upstairs, not the Basement. I do live shows and photo shoots." She looks at me with dark eyes, daring me to ask what a photo shoot is. But before I can, she continues, "My picture is often in ads in newspapers and magazines."

I haven't decided what I want to be when I grow up yet, but I'm certainly hoping to be famous, and the thought that Sylvia DeStephano already has her picture in the paper gives me a dizzy kind of defeated feeling in my head and stomach. She isn't even smart, but there she is, experiencing a "lights, camera, action!" kind of life while I go home to cookies and milk in our small apartment with an occasional trip to Woolworth's.

Sylvia's watching my reaction to her fame with a smirk of Cheshire-cat satisfaction on her face. I want to ask why she can't, you know, just change her clothes after she leaves school and not make it all so obvious to us, and why she is so foolishly attached to material possessions in the first place, but my mouth is too dry to talk.

"Dear God," I pray silently, "I don't think I'm the right choice to save Sylvia. Did You have any idea she's a model?"

God answers immediately. "Of course, my child, I am all-knowing. But remember Bishop O'Brien's words on material possessions. Remember his words on pride. You studied them for more reasons than you realize. Be strong."

I first learned about pride, one of the seven deadlies, from Sister Louise, who continues to warn the class, and me in particular, about it so often.

"It is evil to show off and to call attention to yourself when you are just a speck in comparison to God," Sister Louise tells us over and over, marching up and down our rows of desks and giving me a certain stare, know what I mean, when she passes by.

More than once Sister Louise pulls me out of class after I've just won a spelling or a math bee. "You hurt Jesus and his Father by drawing people's attention to you and your tiny accomplishments, Bridget, when they should be thinking about Him. And you hurt yourself. Remember 'Thou shalt put no false gods before me?'" Sister questions, her mouth drawn into a minus sign. "Don't you think that applies to math problems? To spelling?"

I have, in fact, just about memorized the section in the *Guide* on pride. Pride is the excessive love of one's own excellence. It is one of the seven capital sins; some say it is the blackest because the prideful person—adult or child—puts himself above Almighty God. The sinful, prideful person stubbornly refuses to submit to God's will. His attitude has something Satanic in it.

I find this discussion of pride particularly rhythmic for jumping rope to, which helps me remember the words so the next time Sister quizzes me, I can show I've been studying humility. I begin attacking my pride at its root and stop telling my parents or anyone in my family about my accomplishments in school. I also slow my pace in my reading comprehension tests so that someone else can be tempted into the sin of pride and finish first, but then Sister scolds me for laziness. I have brains, she tells me, and am supposed to try my best, which usually means doing better than everyone else. I'm just not supposed to take any pride or pleasure in my accomplishments. This is what it means to be a Child of God. Everything you do, you do for Him. Any glory, joy, pleasure, sense of satisfaction isn't yours to feel. Even if you've earned it. It belongs to Him. Especially if you're a girl.

Sylvia, chin in the air, wearing tapestry clothing, smiling condescendingly at me, seems to be in the full grips of her deadly sin. She is so prideful that she doesn't even notice, so excessive is her love of her own excellence. She is certainly not conflicted like I've become. The whole situation seems to have something Satanic in it cuz Sylvia appears perfectly happy with herself the way she is. To anyone who's read the *Guide*, that kind of happiness is definitely a sign that something is very wrong.

St. Michael's parish is blessed to have Bishop O'Brien himself as our pastor, since he's in charge of a whole diocese and is much higher in rank than an average pastor. Even though he's a busy man, he visits our parish school quite frequently, going from classroom to classroom to bless the students. They say that he's particularly concerned for the souls of children, which, I suppose, is why he wrote the *Guide*.

Bishop O'Brien's eyes are small and set far back in his head with age, but they're still piercingly bright blue. He looks like he can see everything inside us, even if he can't see much on the outside, know what I mean? He's old and frail and bumps his bishop's staff into just about everything when he walks to the front of our classroom. We're supposed to be grateful for his visits, but really everyone is petrified.

When he arrives, we have to instantly stop what we're doing, quickly stand up, and say, "Good morning, Bishop O'Brien," in a particularly singsong-y kind of way. Then he mumbles something into his robes—no one can tell whether it's English or Latin—and raises a hand to bless us. That's our rosary cue.

All the students in our class have been given a set of rosary beads and we recite a decade every morning. Each decade is a different color to help us keep track of our prayers. To many the colors seemed arbitrary, but I've cracked the code. Blue on Mondays cuz everyone is sad to be back at school. Green on Tuesdays, the day test results are given back, and there's a lot of jealousy. Red on Wednesdays, which is Prince Spaghetti Day. Yellow on Thursdays, when we count up our mission money to buy pagan babies, who are usually Asian. And black on Fridays to commemorate the day Jesus died.

Because they're our school rosaries—"blessed by Bishop O'Brien for special use in school only"—we're forbidden to ever bring them home, and we must produce them in dramatic unison whenever the bishop appears. After Bishop O'Brien's mumble, each of us, at exactly the same instant, has to noiselessly extract our rosaries from their pink plastic cases in our desks, grasp them in our right hands, and stretch our right arms out in front of us so that he can see our rosaries all displayed symmetrically.

We show the bishop our rosaries because they're supposed to be our most valued religious possession. "Rosaries are formed in a circle to symbolize God's unending love for us, a circle that—unless you fall into a state of mortal sin—can never be broken," Sister Louise told us solemnly the day she handed them out.

We are to keep our sacred rosaries raised throughout the bishop's blessing and remain completely quiet with our heads down. But we also have to glance discreetly up to see when he's stopped the blessing cuz his voice is so soft that it's often hard to know. Once we're absolutely sure he's finished, we must say in unison, "Thank you, Bishop O'Brien," and keep our arms raised with our rosaries dangling and our heads lowered until he leaves the room.

Sister Louise goes over this routine with us many times, and we gradually realize how much practice it takes to learn something that will appear to be completely spontaneous.

It is essential, Sister Louise reminds us, that our rosary raising in adoration of God look totally unplanned to the bishop when he enters the room. In this way he'll come to see us as holy and want to return to bless us again. And a blessing from a bishop, who is, after all, pretty high up in the Catholic hierarchy, is potent stuff and not that easy for the average person to come by.

During the first weeks of school, Sister Louise often leaps up from her desk, puts her hand to where her ear is likely to be behind her habit, and exclaims, "Is that a knock I hear on the door?" She rushes down the room, waving her hands all over the place.

It takes us a while to catch on that whenever Sister jumps with excessive animation, she's just pretending to hear a knock in order to give us rosary-raising practice. I start to notice further clues that the bishop's visit isn't real, that this is practice on the q.t. Like when Sister gets to the classroom door, she calls out loudly and with an exaggerated tone of pleasure, which isn't at all like her regular voice or her normal disposition, "Oh. It's Bishop O'Brien. Class? Class! Good mo-o-rning, Bi-shop O'Bri-i-en."

It is then that even the dullest of us realizes that Sister's staging a rehearsal for a visit and that we're already doomed. Sister Louise turns from the classroom door, still smiling expectantly, finds us looking bewildered or trying to get our rosaries out of our desks, and her face instantly transforms from its false serenity to its more natural chalk-white fury. With eyebrows furrowed and teeth clenched, she screams at us, "Where are your rosaries? How will you show the bishop, when he does honor you with a visit, that you are children of God and not of the Devil?"

During one of Bishop O'Brien's visits, I grab my rosary out of my desk with my right hand, thrust it high into the air, and lower my head. My timing is perfect and I feel quite proud. But then something so horrible happens that I'm convinced God has let go of me just the way He abandoned mankind after we fell into sin in Paradise (all because of a snake). A link in the middle of the black decade of my rosary has broken. One end slowly slithers out of my sweaty hand and hangs straight down. It begins to sway sacrilegiously from side to side. The circle is broken.

Sylvia notices immediately and smiles menacingly at me, her eyes narrow with scheming. She raises her left hand and frantically waves it about. I know she wants Bishop O'Brien to call on her so she can tell him right then and there about my broken rosary. But, thank God, the bishop never calls on people, probably cuz he can't really see clearly past the front row. He just makes an extra sign of the cross in our direction and walks out.

I pray to God during our morning rosary decade to do something to stop Sylvia. I know it's a mortal sin to ask specifically for her to fall off a runway and break her neck or to be strangled by someone pulling off a shirt too quickly when she has a fast change backstage, or at least blinded by too many flashcubes going off all at once when she steps out onto the runway, so while I secretly hope for any of these things to happen, I don't dare to actually pray for them. I ask God simply to dispose of Sylvia in any way that He, in His infinite wisdom, thinks best. I vow to be good if only He can do something to stop her.

Sylvia then proceeds to tell me that she'll take her time letting Sister Louise know about my rosary, saying that it's much more fun watching me worry for a while. But I know that God, in actuality, is intervening in her change of heart. She plans to reveal everything right before a big spelling test we're having in a week's time, but her modeling suddenly increases. Being in school less and thinking about her adornments more takes her mind off me. And I thank God for a second time.

Right before Halloween, when Bishop O'Brien is visiting us and we're lifting our rosaries to him, God answers my prayers a third time in His own special—and what I'm discovering can be quite dramatic—way. As Sylvia raises her rosary, the cross falls off. It bounces on the floor and lands against my chair leg. This is God's special sign to Sylvia and me—*for you as children are most capable of seeing God's signs*—and its interpretation is immediately clear.

The cross has literally moved away from Sylvia and toward me, which can mean only one thing— God is on my side now. But I know that in showing Himself to me in such an obvious way, God expects me to do my part. He wants what He asked of me a while ago now: to exorcize the Devil from Sylvia, to bring her soul back to Him, and to do it all on the q.t.

"Sylvia," I whisper while the bishop prays over the class, "God's abandoned you," and I point to her cross. She moves to pick it up, but I block her with my foot. "Why do you think He landed against my chair?" She looks afraid. I'm tempted then and there to chastise her vanity and pride, her love of material goods, her state of sin so excessive that she isn't even upset by it. But I remember that God's waiting for me to act.

To rid Sylvia of the Devil. To perform my first exorcism. My mother cast the Devil out of my room by saying some prayers from her missal and sprinkling a lot of holy water, neither of which I have at the moment. I swallow hard. My knowledge of the *Guide* and my Bible stories will have to do. I know that an exorcist can't make physical contact with the possessed. Well, everyone knows that. And I've been careful, these past few weeks, never to touch Sylvia. Still, I move a step away from her, to the farther side of my desk.

Bishop O'Brien finishes his prayer. "Thank you, Bi-shop O-Bri-en," the class calls out.

"Sylvia," I say softly, "listen. I know about God's signs. Your clothes. Adornments. It's all vanity. He's asked me to help." She looks amazed, then at her little cross, still against my chair. I can feel that the time has come.

The bishop is walking around the whole classroom, giving us an extra blessing against Halloween spirits. I check that no one is watching us. "I cast you out, oh evil one!" I whisper, pointing at Sylvia's heart with my rosary-free hand. "Leave the body and mind of Sylvia DeStephano. Give her peace!"

Sister is fussing around the bishop, helping him with his staff. "Take away her deadly sins of pride and vanity!" I forget what the other five deadlies are but figure He'll get the message.

Bishop O'Brien is getting nearer to us, so Sylvia raises her right arm with her rosary higher out in front of her, like we're supposed to, and I move my arm up as well. We're both carefully concealing the broken parts of our rosaries in our fists. I mouth the words, "Depart from her," but in my head, I'm bellowing them out so I know God and the devil can hear me. And then I have to speak silently because Sister Louise is so close. *Let no love of adornments, or purple shoes, or tapestry clothing, or pink nail polish be left when you depart!* My soundless voice is deep and resonant. I glance to check how Sylvia is doing, and she looks pretty pale. Clearly, I've roused Satan. He's probably moving around a lot inside her now. *Beelzebub! Be gone!* I scream out mutely, hoping that, in the spirit world, I sound like an experienced exorcist. Satan probably doesn't even know it's just me and thinks it's the bishop or at least a high-ranking nun. As Bishop O'Brien leaves, Sylvia suddenly begins to make odd gulping sounds. Like she's choking or maybe about to throw up.

She's crying. But much more than that. Her tears are black—definitely a sign of evil. I remember the words from the *Guide* exactly. *And Jesus expelled evil spirits from their black souls.* I'm more confident now and while I still don't dare touch her, I stare into Sylvia, willing the Devil to exit from her body.

The more she cries, the blacker the tears get. The spirits could take any form. I know what this means. I've done it! The Devil and his demons are being exorcised from Sylvia. And the spirits are exiting through her eyes. I only hope that they'll stay in the form of tears and not stretch into long hissing snakes.

Sylvia pulls some perfectly folded pink tissues from her sleeve and smears the traces of evil all over her cheeks. For someone who's just experienced an exorcism, based on all I've read, she's taking it pretty well.

"Sylvia," I murmur in the spirit of God's forgiveness, "I won't tell about your crucifix. Don't tell about my rosary." She nods. I pick up her cross and place it on her desk.

By the end of the school day, I'm only half convinced that my interpretation of Sylvia's cross falling off had anything to do with God being on my side. And there still remains the disturbing fact that my own rosary is broken. Is God telling me that while we're forbidden to take our rosaries home, I can bend the rule for one night because I performed an exorcism today? I'm not sure, but I still slip mine into my school bag for my mother to fix on the q.t.

When I get home, I'll have to tell my mother everything that's been going on with Sylvia and me and our rosaries, even though Sister Louise has forbidden us to talk about school matters at home. I want my own mother to understand the depths of my fears for the past weeks that Bishop O'Brien and Sister Louise might have discovered my broken rosary. She should also know about Sylvia's modeling career, and her pridefulness, and about how much worse Sylvia's pride was than the pride that threatened my own soul earlier this year. And mostly I have to explain how today's signs from God—through Sylvia's rosary—that He's on my side led me to just perform my first exorcism. This is something I know she'll appreciate since she was the one who cast Satan and his snakes out of my bedroom. We still never let that holy water font get empty.

But once I'm in our light yellow and white, freshly painted kitchen, with a nice woody smell from the plywood cabinets my mother is slowly building, I can't think where to start, and the words get caught in my stomach.

"I could get in trouble, you know, for having a broken rosary and for bringing it out of the classroom," I begin.

My mother takes the rosary from me and looks at it carefully. "This is so cheaply made. No wonder it's falling apart. I'm sure that's why Sister doesn't want any of you to bring your rosaries home," she says matter-of-factly.

"That isn't it!" How can my mother be so unaware of God's powers? "God shows Himself in signs through our rosaries. We aren't supposed to touch them, except when we pray. Especially someone like me, who, as Sister Louise is always ready to remind me, is so often in a prideful state of near deadly sin about subtraction problems and sometimes spelling bees."

As if she didn't hear me at all, my mother puts the rosary on the counter and suggests that I have some cookies and milk. We wash our hands and go to the table.

"Bridget," she says somewhat sternly, "there's such a large group of kids in your class that Sister must feel she can only control them by fear. But," and she grasps my face in her hands, "you mustn't take this business of 'signs' and 'deadly sins' and 'pride' all so seriously. It's just meant to make the kids behave."

My father always says that you're not as good a Catholic if you didn't go to Catholic school, and now I can see exactly what he means cuz my mother—who went to public school—just isn't getting it.

"Now for that rosary," she smiles, and fixes it in about ten seconds with a pair of pliers. I get up and start to swing the rosary around, rejoicing that I'm back in the circle of God's love. "Don't be so rough or it could break again," my mother warns.

"Okay. No problem." I put the rosary back in its case and into my book bag. Even though she's not being very sympathetic, I decide that I still have to tell her everything about Sylvia right now. She'll believe me when she gets all the details, you know. After all, she did a great job with the rosary.

"About a month ago, Mommy, I discovered that Sylvia DeStephano was suffering from the deadly sin of pride. She's been possessed for a while now, and God gave me signs that He expected me to cast out her demons."

My mother stops me. "Bridget, what did I just say? Both you and Sylvia are much too young to be as sinful as you imagine." She goes into my bedroom and comes out with the *Guide*. "I found this today under your pillow when I was changing your bed. It's unhealthy for a child your age—or any age—to be reading morbid and superstitious material like this. It says it's written in commemoration of Vatican II, but it sounds more like it's from the Middle Ages. It's a regular guide to witch-hunting and I won't have it." She opens up to a page I've bent back and begins to read aloud. "*Jesus gave all believers the power to cast out demons... You, too, my children, can have that power.*" She shudders, then looks intently at me. "Children don't have the power to cast out demons."

"But I do have that power," I protest, starting to cry. "I exorcized Satan from Sylvia this afternoon," I yell. Why doesn't she believe me? "The Devil was very responsive to my voice. He and his demons came right out of her eyes." I try to speak with just as much conviction as my mother has even though I'm crying because I don't see how she can't trust me about something as important as this, even if she didn't go to Catholic school.

When I reach inside my pocket to get something to wipe my eyes, I pull out one of Sylvia's blackened pink tissues that I must have picked up by mistake. I throw the tissue onto the floor and run to the far corner of the kitchen, slipping on a pile of wood shavings from my mother's cabinet making, and I scream and scream and scream. My mother rushes over to me and holds me tightly.

"Bridey! What is it?" she keeps repeating.

"It's the proof," I murmur. "When the demons came out, Sylvia cried black tears. You can see some of them on that piece of pink evil."

My mother walks over to pick up the stained tissue. "Don't touch it!" I shout. "It's black because it's the Devil!"

She sighs. "It's black, but it has nothing whatsoever to do with the Devil." Still fingering the tissue, she says, "Now that surprises me. The nuns are so strict. Even with her modeling."

"What are you surprised at?" I yell. My mother turns to me, about to cry herself. She sits on the floor next to me, even though it's germy, and holds my hands.

"That they'd let Sylvia wear mascara to school." She pulls me to her. "Bridey, I'm sorry. That's what it is."

I jerk away. "So you're saying it's makeup and not the Devil that came out of Sylvia's eyes this afternoon?"

"Yes." My mother tries to hug me again. "Bridget, we don't even know if the Devil or demons have ever been known to exit a body through someone's eyes, but if they have, I doubt they're going to come out of any little girls we know."

But then I notice it—my holy water font on the doorframe of my bedroom right next to the kitchen—and instantly none of what I'm saying is ridiculous. I get up and move away from my mother. "Why don't you believe me?" I cry out, going over to the font. I dip my finger in it and flick some holy water at her. "You're the one who cast the Devil out of my bedroom! How can you not have faith in me? If you can perform an exorcism, why can't I?"

My mother doesn't say anything for a long time, and she won't look at me.

"What about me?" I scream. "What about the Devil that was in my room? What about Satan and his snakes that woke me up? That made me pull my hair? I'm a little girl and the Devil was after me. And you got him to leave me alone. What about all of that? What about me?"

My mother just sits there on the floor, looking so sad. "Bridget, honey?" she pats the floor for me to sit beside her. But I won't budge. She leans her head back, then speaks so quietly. "You were a special case, honey. You're my little girl. A mother has to take extra care of her own child. I'd do anything to help you, you know that, right? I'd always fight whatever you thought was hurting you."

What is my mother saying? I can't be sure. She's crying now. But I have to get out of the house. I can't let her say anything else.

I unlock my bike slowly, going over every word of my mother's. The rosaries break cuz they're poorly made. I was a special case. Sylvia cried black cuz her mascara was running. We're too young to be guilty of deadly sins. I was a special case. The class is large. Sister has to control by fear. Nothing means anything other than what it is.

I'm angry and confused, so I pedal my bike up Sherman Street hill as hard as I can. Part of me wants Sylvia's face to grow pale tomorrow when she sees my intact rosary, to think that God has performed another miracle. But part of me doesn't want her to ever be as afraid as she looked today or as afraid as I used to be of Satan's snakes under my bed. I reach the top of the hill and turn, pedaling as fast as I can for the descent. About halfway down, with the wind blowing through my hair and cooling my damp neck, I let go of the handlebars and stop pedaling. Like I always do. Riding fast down Sherman Hill is one of my favorite things in all the world. My parents hate me doing it. They say I could get myself killed. But I'm not afraid. Not of bikes and cars at any rate. I feel the wind drying my lips and my stomach unclenching.

I'll do what I always do. Wait for a sign. If I can ride all the way to Garden Street without having to pedal, that'll be a message from God that Sylvia is just a stupid, vain girl who wears makeup when she's still too young. But if I have to pedal, then I'll have proof that the Devil was in her after all, just like he'd been in my room, and that it took me to cast him out of Sylvia today.

The car comes out of nowhere. It's going slowly, but I'm not paying attention. I'm thinking of Sylvia's mascara tissues, of my hair-pulling, of how my mother, not God, fixed my rosary today. Of how my mother fixes everything in our house, even Satan. I almost lose control of my bike as I brake hard and jump off.

Oh, God. It's my father. He can see that I'm fine. But he's angry. "Bridget?" he yells. "How often do we have to tell you not to ride with no hands? I'll have a few choice words for you, missy, when you get home. Now walk that bike the rest of the way." And he starts to drive off. Then he stops and pushes his head out the window and shouts, "On the sidewalk!"

I can't believe my bad luck. Now I'll never know the truth about Sylvia.

6. At the Kitchen Window II:
The Bike Fight Story

My father's place, every night at dinner, is at our kitchen window. I wish they'd shut it before we sat down—and drawn the curtains—cuz everyone in the neighborhood must be listening to him yell at my mother and me. Our three-family houses are so close together, and most kids are out riding their bikes or just strolling around. They only have to look up and, since my mother keeps that window so clean, watch him flail his arms or bang his dinner plate with his fork. Who knows why he's acting quite so mental. The neighbors might even see that piece of spinach hanging out of his mouth on the window side. Just dangling there—how can he not feel it?— like the end of a worm trying to slither away. As if dinner wasn't already disgusting enough.

"She probably still rides her bike all the time without holding on. I'm at work, you're at home, and I expect you to supervise the child. But do you?" He's not just shouting. He's acting like I'm not in the room. Sometimes he treats my mother and me like we're total idiots.

'Course she isn't completely in my good books these days either. Because, for a family with a lot of secrets, I'm being denied my fair share of them. Between the exorcism and getting caught riding downhill with no hands, I've lost all rights to any privacy in our house. My parents demand to be told everything I do. In school and at home. If a patron saint of privacy existed, I'd be organizing novenas in her honor for months at a time—never mind the usual nine days—and definitely, absolutely, in secret. But I can't find a privacy saint in my Bible Stories book. There's Jude for lost causes, and Rita for loneliness. But no privacy. Typical, know what I mean?

"What do you expect?" my mother snaps back. "For me to chase her all over the place?"

"Why don't you believe me?" I moan. We've been having this conversation for over fifteen minutes and many months. "I'm not going to risk my immortal soul over how I ride my bike." I actually have stopped riding with no hands, despite that lovely sensation of the wind on me as I sped down hills with my arms at my sides.

"I am obeying you, even though I don't want to!" I grumble, but neither of them seems to hear me, you know? The worm finally wriggles back into his mouth.

My parents have been arguing about my bike since way before they bought it for me, and they love to tell people "the bike fight story." Apparently it lasted for about a year, with each of them uttering exactly the same lines. You might think they'd learn a lesson from that. But no.

One day I got involved in the bike fight. I remember none of this, and it clearly should be a family secret cuz it embarrasses me in ways I still don't fully understand and is definitely a major invasion of my privacy.

THE BIKE FIGHT STORY

MOTHER: "We have to buy her a two-wheeler because everyone else in the neighborhood has one, and she can't be expected to go around on her tricycle forever." ('Course I wasn't, by then, actually riding my tricycle. I was six years old and didn't want to look like a complete idiot.)

FATHER: "She can't have a two-wheeler because she'll fall off the bike and lose her virginity."

BRIDGET: (After listening to this fight for ages and desperately wanting a bike, I come out of my room in tears.) "I don't know what my virginity is, but I promise not to lose it, even if I do fall off my bike."

When they first told me the story, I understood immediately that my line was the joke. I knew it would be the part where everyone would laugh. Even though I didn't get it.

Three years from when I first allegedly uttered that line, I still don't have the full picture of what my virginity is. I mean I think, generally speaking, it's about sex, but there's absolutely no way I can figure out what a bicycle has to do with it or how, if a girl fell off her bike, her virginity would go missing—without any boys around and with all her clothes still on. So I wonder if maybe some other kind of virginity exists that I haven't yet discovered.

I realize that being a virgin is what makes the Blessed Virgin Mother special. But surely, she didn't have a bicycle. Though, if I've been blessed with the BVM's kind of virginity—the variety you can misplace all on your own and fully clothed—then logically I'm going to be chosen by God to do something important, probably in the near future since Mary was very young when she became the mother of Jesus. Not that I haven't done a fair bit already for a person my age. But no doubt it's something that'll get me a lot more credit than the exorcism did. And when that happens no one will laugh anymore.

I hate these fights, but at least they prevent my parents from noticing that after chewing my red meat until my jaw is tired, I spit it into my paper napkin. Cuz it's impossible to swallow. While we're cleaning the table, I grab my napkin on the q.t. and stuff it deep in the garbage basket. That meat is my own little secret.

But one night, after cramming an unusually full napkin into the trash, I walk over to the window. It's so dark that all I can see is my own reflection. And in an instant I'm terrified. What if I'm just an average girl? No angels coming with any special announcements for me. No distinction by God as someone exceptional or unusual in any way. No special kind of virginity.

My mother touches my shoulder and says I look pale. Like I'm catching a cold. That I should take a bath early and get into bed to ward it off. Not even bother with my homework. She'll write a note for school.

7. Holy Cards, Spiritual Bouquets, Relics, Indulgences and Other Divine Materials

I'm so glad we ended up getting my missal from the Green Stamps catalogue, even though it took twenty-five thousand stamps, cuz it's way bigger and more beautiful than the one at the Catholic store. Each page is bright white and almost as thin as tissue paper, but it also contains many thick, shiny-colored pictures with photos of the Sacred Heart, the Blessed Virgin, and many martyrs being tortured. Those pictures are what first give me the idea of inserting my holy card collection into my missal. I file them carefully, matching up the cards with their saints like, say, St. Patrick with the page in my missal that's his Saint Day (March 17).

My favorite holy cards and the most blessed of all are the touched-to-a-relic holy cards. They're double-sided and have a circle about an eighth of an inch cut out in the center front under the saint's picture. From this circle, a bit of fabric shows through that's pasted between the two sides. And right under the fabric dot, it says "Touched to a Relic of Saint Stephen" or Saint Joan of Arc, or whoever. I so wanted to have a Virgin Mary "touched-to" holy card, but understand that because she was assumed—body and soul—into heaven, she obviously couldn't leave any bones behind to become relics for fabric to be touched to. But my mother managed to find me a Virgin Mary "touched to a relic of the Veil of Our Lady of Loreto" card. So her clothes are used as relics since there aren't any bones! You have to admit that Catholics are so clever to figure all of this out. Right now I have eleven touched-to cards, but my mother says that she'll be able to get me more soon.

The fabric that touches the relic is usually a deep green, purple, or red, but sometimes it can be yellow-gold, or pastel pink, or blue. It has taken me a couple of years to build up the courage to touch the fabric that had been touched-to-a-relic-of. But my friend Lucy, for reasons I can't explain, goes way further. She licks the tip of her finger and makes tiny, circular motions on the holy relic fabric so that it gets a little wet, and then she actually puts her finger back into her mouth. She says she's trying to suck all the relicky goodness into herself, and she wants me to try. I don't, though, because I'm afraid it might be sacrilegious. And possibly germy. Or that it could use up all the goodness. And perhaps mostly because it reminds me of The Holy in the holy water—very potent, but never to be put in your mouth.

'Course it's always so hard to know exactly what to do. There's a fine line between worship and sin that it seems a lot of saints crossed, but the rest of us can't. I mean, whenever I think about St. Agnes's not bathing ever in her whole life, even if it was from a divine modesty, and never wanting the air— let alone anyone who might be looking, like a parent, a relative, or even a bug that just happened to be flying by—to see her body, she seems sinful rather than holy. Maybe even a bit insane, you know?

Over the entrance to our bathroom we have a white plaque my mother bought from the Catholic store that says "Cleanliness is next to Godliness." So I guess wherever St. Agnes is in heaven, she isn't at the right hand of God, or at least she's upwind from him.

Rules are so confusing here on earth. When Lucy's black cat, which I sometimes think is a manifestation of Satan, killed a bird in our backyard two years ago, it took my parents days to decide if they'd let us give it a Christian burial. How could making a shoebox coffin, sprinkling it with holy water, singing a hymn or two while processing around the yard, burying it, and marking its grave with a cross be wrong in any possible way? But my parents told me it wasn't clear whether animals had souls and whether actually blessing the bird would be right. I had to be very forceful with them, which I rarely am cuz conflict in our house is hardly something to be encouraged. But, in this case, I felt I was doing God's work.

I think what finally convinced them was my incessant singing of the hymn "God Sees the Little Sparrow Fall," especially the line, "If God so loves the little birds, I know He loves me too," which Anne taught me for my First Holy Communion when I was seven. And even though it's a Protestant hymn, I remember thinking what a lovely present it was for her to give me. Teaching someone a special song is so original.

But I also remember that Grandpa started to look like he was about to have one of Uncle Johnny's seizures as I sang it swaggering around the house in my Holy Communion outfit, tossing my head to make my veil swish and doing a little tap dance on the linoleum in the kitchen with my noisy, white patent leather shoes. He almost refused to come to the church for the ceremony.

"She's not fit to receive the sacrament!" he yelled. "She's singing the words of heretics!" Both my parents had to sit him down, and I think my mother put some whisky in his coffee to get him to agree finally that I wasn't a heathen and wouldn't be eternally damned if I received my Holy Communion without going to confession for singing a Protestant hymn.

In the end, my parents let us bury the bird, read some words from my father's missal, and sing the hymn, but it had to be totally on the q.t. I wasn't allowed to invite any funeral guests or have pallbearers, which they always do for a funeral at St. Michael's. My parents and I marched around the yard with the bird in a shoebox, and my father buried "the dear departed," then covered it with dirt and marked its grave with a cross my mother had made from sticks and some black yarn. I thought the ceremony was beautiful, but I could see that my parents weren't quite comfortable with it. Always that fine line between the sacred and the sinful.

I first started getting touched-to-a-relic holy cards when they appeared rather mysteriously for me in mail addressed to my mother. She said they came as a thank-you gift for one's child from a special order of priests, the Slaves of the Immaculate Heart of Mary, in Still River, Massachusetts, from whom she bought Spiritual Bouquets. Spiritual Bouquets are for people who've died, which we bring to their wakes and later to their death anniversary Masses. They promise that the priests of the Slaves of the Immaculate Heart of Mary will say a certain number of Masses for the repose of the soul of the dead person. The price of a Spiritual Bouquet varies, depending both on how many Masses you buy and on how decorative the actual card is. Some of those Spiritual Bouquets are pretty amazing. They're padded and covered in moiré or satin—fabrics I know about cuz my mother uses tiny remnants of them that she gets on fabulous sales to make beautiful Infant of Prague outfits.

My mother does buy Spiritual Bouquets from the "upper line," so naturally they're the most expensive, which causes problems between her and my father. He says you could just get a plain card with as many Masses and spend about half the amount of money. "It's bad enough to pay priests to say Masses in the first place since that's their job, but to pay them to make extravagant cards is blasphemous." But my mother feels that a plain card is insufficiently respectful of the living as well as the dead. "If you're giving a family Masses for their loved one's immortal soul, you should at least present them with a beautiful 'bouquet.'"

Just looking at those gorgeous Spiritual Bouquets, with their fancy writing based on genuine reproductions of illuminated manuscripts, you know that people who receive them are way more likely to get into heaven than people who don't. I'm sure they resemble invitations rich people send to their fancy parties or weddings. But with Spiritual Bouquets, regular, ordinary folks who might even be kind of poor get to have a beautiful invitation to the most important place in the world. And people my parents know always seem to have some relation who just died, so my mother keeps a number of Spiritual Bouquets on hand. Just in case. I'm not allowed to touch them or even open the drawer in the credenza where she hides them, each in its own envelope and then wrapped individually in expensive, thick plastic wrap.

So I content myself with just fingering and thinking about licking the touched-to-a-relic holy cards. Keeping holy cards in my missal turns out to be a smarter idea than I'd initially realized because looking at them during Mass gives me something to do that doesn't count as misbehaving when I'm not actually paying attention.

After the relic holy cards, my next favorite are indulgence holy cards. These cards have short prayers on them that, when repeated, help people get days taken off their required stay in purgatory. The little prayer or "indulgence" is always printed on the back of the card. 'Course if it's a touched-to-a-relic card, I don't even bother about the indulgence cuz it's already at my highest ranking level and therefore filed differently in my missal. But if it's just a regular indulgence holy card, then I rank it by the number of days the indulgence grants. Most are thirty-day indulgences, some sixty or ninety, and a rare few are for one hundred twenty days.

"Indulgences" is like a card game from heaven, and I come from a family of card players, so the game makes perfect sense to me. I play it often, usually during Mass. The basic rules aren't hard: you pick an indulgence card with a particular number, say sixty days; then you choose a person in whose name you're going to offer up the indulgence, say Grandpa Flaherty, who died a few months ago; and finally you decide on the number of indulgence reps you're going to do, say ten; and that determines how many days off from purgatory the person gets. If I say a sixty-day indulgence ten times for Grandpa, that means he gets six hundred days taken off his required stay in purgatory.

At this point in my life and for reasons I don't understand, I believed that people could not spend a longer time in purgatory than their age and that you could say indulgences for the living, which they could bank and save for when they died. So I could always figure out exactly how many indulgences I needed to cover a person's whole life, assuming I liked them and didn't want them wasting any of their afterlife in purgatory.

As one boring sermon follows another, I busily calculate indulgences. In one Mass, depending on the indulgences I choose and on the length of the sermon, I can recite all the indulgences I need to get myself, my parents, grandparents, and, often, various friends, extended family members, and pets out of purgatory free. I thoroughly enjoy the challenge of figuring out someone's age and then determining the number of indulgences they need. But I'm not greedy. I don't just go for the one-hundred-twenty-day indulgences, though you only need three per year of these, so they're very good for grandparents or for pets whose age has to be multiplied by large amounts to be calculated in human terms or if you're just in a hurry.

I prefer to mix the indulgences up cuz I'm sure that God—after helping me get my missal free of charge, even if some of what it actually says is pretty disturbing, especially about husbands and wives—is listening to me and appreciates hearing those little prayers in different and unexpected combinations. So there I am during the sermon or, if I've gotten really involved, even into the consecration, calculating indulgences. For a year, you need approximately 12 thirty-day indulgences (one for each month of the year); or 6 sixty-day ones (half the months in a year); or four ninety-day indulgences (one for every three months of the year); or just three one-hundred-twenty-day indulgences (one for every four months of the year).

I start with my Grandpa, who died so recently. He was eighty years old. So he can go straight to heaven if I say 80 x 12 or 960 thirty-day indulgences, 80 x 6 or 480 sixty-day indulgences, 80 x 4 or 320 ninety-day indulgences. Or if I say only 80 x 3 or 240 one-hundred-twenty-day indulgences, which, for the purposes of time and because of his age and because I have to pray for other people besides him, is often what I have to resort to, you know—but just for him.

I then usually move on to my mother, who is somewhere between forty and forty-one, about half

Grandpa's age. She can totally eliminate her stay in Purgatory if I can make my way through approximately 40 x 12 or 480 thirty-day indulgences, 40 x 6 or 240 sixty-day indulgences, 40 x 4 or 160 ninety-day indulgences, or if I say only 40 x 3 or 120 one-hundred-twenty-day indulgences. I like the symmetry of saying 120 one-hundred-twenty-day indulgences, but worry that this pleasure is a temptation by Satan for me to give in to what looks clever but is in reality just the lazy man's way of indulgence praying—saying the least for the most.

I know that God would not approve of such a "glib" (a new word I recently learned in my accelerated vocab class) way of praying, especially for a person who isn't old like Grandpa was. My mother can also be saved if I mix it up and say approximately 48 thirty-day indulgences (four years), 72 sixty-day indulgences (12 years), 40 ninety-day indulgences (ten years), and 48 one-hundred-twenty-day indulgences (15.5 years).

There is, of course, an almost infinite number of combinations, and cuz I do this in church and am supposed to be praying—which I still am—but not solving math problems—which I also most definitely am doing—I have to perform all of the calculations in my head, memorize them, and then count off the indulgences. Frequently I try to use a number of different indulgences within a particular grouping. So I might be saying three different thirty-day indulgences, each eighteen times; six different sixty-day indulgences, each twelve times; four different ninety-day indulgences, each ten times; and two different one-hundred-twenty-day indulgences, each twenty-four times. I feel that this redirection of my apparent pride in my math abilities to serve a religious function could satisfy even Sister Louise.

All of this indulgence recitation and calculation is extremely satisfying, so sometimes I even do it when I'm supposed to be working on my homework. Though I stopped myself after one incident when my father found me with my missal open and indulgence cards around the table while I was studying for a geography test, which led to a difficult and confusing discussion of whether I thought I'd been called by God to a vocation as a nun.

My violent denials contradicted what looked like an excess of devotion, but eventually my mother and I managed to put my "extra praying" down to my apparent anxiety about the impending test. This led my father to give me such a lecture at dinner about the dangers of procrastination that I didn't pray for him for the rest of the week. But when I do rather poorly on the test and he treats me kindly, confessing that his own sense of geography is pretty bad, I put him right back on the top rung of my prayer list.

I also get punished in school for underachieving on that geography test and, perhaps as a warning, am given a very detailed book on the early Christian virgin martyrs. When I start to read it, I can't believe there are so many female saints I've never heard of. As soon as I see what the book is about, I immediately call a meeting of my friends Agnes and Lucy, and we find over fifty really interesting virgin martyrs—Agatha, Monica, Anne, Helena, Ursula, Eulalia, even Agnes. Lucy says we'll have enough material for playing what we now call Fallen Saint Stories until we're old and married. We actually learn a lot of grown-up material from that book about the many abuses of female body parts, especially forcing the virgins to display their breasts and then cutting them off, making them walk around in public with no clothes on or ripping flesh off them in various places so that their bones showed through (in obvious anticipation of being made into relics). And threatening their virginity, which they all fought and died to keep.

These are all things they definitely don't tell you on holy cards or in my Bible Stories book. And Agnes, who bakes a lot with her mother and who has started wearing a bra, even though she definitely doesn't need it, keeps threatening that for one of our birthdays, she's going to make "virgin martyr breast cupcakes." She'll ice them in white, with a Hershey's kiss on the top, red (blood-soaked) napkins underneath, and serve them on a silver platter, like many of the virgin martyrs were—including her own namesake, St. Agnes. But so far she never has.

It is, in the end, not geography, or virgin martyrs, but vocabulary that destroys the sense of balance I've been feeling—with my family, with God, and just in general—ever since I got my missal at the Green Stamps store. It happens during Lent.

Whenever we start a different vocabulary list, Sister Francis Xavier puts the new words on the board and goes around the room to see if we know any of their meanings. When it's my turn to guess a meaning, the word I'm given, a word that I not only do not know the definition of, but that puts my faith into dire question, is "plenary." I've seen the word many times, I admit to Sister. A number of my holy cards say "plenary indulgence" on them.

"Welll-la?" she overly enunciates so that I can see the ugly underside of her pointed tongue. I imagined the term meant something like "plenty of" indulgences and decided from the beginning not to allow any of these vague cards into the important pages of my missal. I keep them all in the index on the grounds that they're insufficiently clear for the precise kinds of calculations I do.

When Sister Francis explains that one, just one (one!) plenary indulgence is good for a lifetime—

meaning that if it is said only once, it could let someone who is ninety-seven years old out of purgatory just as readily as it can get a two-year-old out—I suddenly feel that God has been making some kind of fool of me when all the while I've been thinking we were back on such good terms. There I've been, perfecting my multiplication and division skills for what I thought was the saving of my and my family's and friends' and pets' immortal souls, when I could have said only one plenary indulgence—one per person or pet—for everybody I know and want to pray for and maybe even for some I'm not so wild about.

Are plenary indulgences made for the mathematically illiterate? Or am I the illiterate one for using the limited-expiration-date indulgences without further investigating all my options? Have I been precipitous in my praying? Overly confident in my numerical abilities? Stealthy in my pretense of being engrossed in the Mass when all the time I was, though praying, also doing something else on the q.t.? Was I selfish in trying to pray for myself and my loved ones? And worse, in saying all of these indulgences and doing the calculations differently every time—cuz, yes, I confess that each day I was at Mass I did do a full set for myself and my parents and grandparents and often my aunts Santa Anna and Maria, and the Staten Island relatives starting with Aunt Eleanor—a sign that I was being prideful again, like Sister Louise used to accuse me all the time, especially about my math abilities?

Also did repeating all those indulgences mean that, deep down, I'm unsure of my faith? Why did I go over different patterns of indulgences every week, knowing that having done one round of them was good for a person's lifetime? Do I secretly question the power of indulgences? Am I, in the end, simply an arithmetical Doubting Thomas? And now that I know about plenary indulgences, can I be converted to the concept of one lifetime indulgence, especially having seen that so many of the plenaries are shorter—some only a single sentence!—than even the thirty-day ones? It doesn't seem fair or just. It seems arbitrary. Whimsical. Even untrue.

And it is at this moment of my uncertainty about indulgences that I begin to wonder if God-the-Father, smiting Pharaoh with all of his chariots and charioteers; if Jesus, resisting temptation on the Mount; if the Holy Spirit, flying around and pooping out flames on everyone's head; if Mary, conceiving of Jesus by an angel through her ear; whether all of them, in some way, or possibly in many ways, are also maybe (though I hate to say this) *fraudulent*.

These questions are too big and too deeply disturbing for me to entertain without feeling like I'll lose my faith entirely. When I go to bed that night, I hear Satan's snakes hissing around on the floor underneath me. They've been quiet for so long. I take their presence as a sign that this doubting is surely a path to my destruction, and I can't talk to anyone about it. What would my mother think of all my indulgence combos and reps said during Mass for months on end? That she had spawned an infidel? Am I worse than a pagan baby? Would she stop loving me?

So the next day, which luckily is a Saturday, I decide to take the easy road. The only one I can find that's a compromise between giving up my faith in God completely and staying in the Church as a good Catholic girl with what I absolutely know I believe in. I have to get rid of those holy cards—of every one with an indulgence on it (except the relic ones because I've never used their indulgences). After breakfast I go to my room and shake all the holy cards out of my missal onto my bed and check—once, twice, thrice (because three is a holy number)—and root out all the indulgence cards, from the thirty-day ones to the plenaries. I don't need to categorize them now. I've decided that they're all tempting me into disbelief, so I need to get rid of them immediately and on the q.t., even before I put the other cards back into my missal.

As I gather up the indulgence holy cards and am about to throw them into the large trash bag with this week's newspapers, I stop and wonder whether they've been blessed. They probably have. If something is blessed—like palm from Palm Sunday—and you want to get rid of it, which I suppose one might want to after a five to twenty-year accumulation, you are ideally supposed to burn it and then bury it, but at least bury it and say a prayer over it about ashes to ashes and dust to dust, etc. While it does seem like I've already lost a lot of my faith, I don't want to add to my sins by mistreating something holy, even if I've been very mistreated by them.

There's only one thing to do. I have to bury them. So I go to the cellar. I rifle around through all sorts of cellar junk looking for my beach pail. Finally I find it under a pile of Christmas decorations. At least my mother's gardening spade is hanging on a rusty nail by the door. I put all the indulgence cards into the bucket and go out to our backyard, under the tree. I want to find a proper resting place for my cards.

'Course now that I'm getting rid of them— casting them out, in the way Jesus did to devils—I start to cry. I've loved my indulgence holy cards so much—every one of them. Even if they weren't relic-touched, they've been touched by me, time and again. And now they're going to be purged. Almost martyred. It seems so sad to put them in the ground where they'll be dark and alone and get dirty and wet when it rains. And where they will eventually disintegrate. I'm having second thoughts about the whole thing when I see the little cross stuck in the ground for the dead bird.

Suddenly, as if the Virgin herself is guiding me by the hand, I know what to do. I'll bury the indulgence cards with the dead bird, which must be just bones now. That is a sanctified place. A holy place. As I pull the cross temporarily out of the ground so I can dig, I realize that I won't mind burying the cards now. Their final resting place will be to surround the relics of a bird, a common sparrow who was taken malevolently before its time, who had done no wrong, but was simply a martyr to the sadistic impulses of Lucy's evil black cat. These holy cards will be touched to the relic of this common bird, and eventually they will materialize before the Special Order of the Priests of the Slaves of the Immaculate Heart of the Spiritual Bouquets. And they will be transformed into touched-to-the-relic cards, the highest of holy cards. And some other little girl will love them above all her other holy cards, and they will be elevated in the eyes of man and the eyes of God.

I don't think I'm ever again going to want to lick a touched-to-the-relic holy card, though I know I'll always love them. My missal will actually be easier to read with fewer holy cards in it. And I plan to read it much more carefully and pay less attention to these cards, which, after all, only touched the bones or clothes of some saint. Before I had a missal to look at, I hadn't quite understood that the readings in church come directly out of the Bible. And the Bible contains the actual words of God. If I read my missal more and my holy cards less and let Him speak to me directly, then surely my doubts will disappear.

It is with great solemnity and singleness of purpose that I bury the indulgence cards in the remains of the box next to the bird, which I try not to touch because it looks disgusting and germy. I repack the earth, replace the cross, and go inside to wash my hands. Once. Twice. Three times. Because three is a holy number. And cuz you never know what's been in that bird.

8. At the Kitchen Window III: Pipe Dreams

I'm having a perfectly lovely time with my Aunt Eleanor from Staten Island, who's sitting in the chair by the freshly washed kitchen window. It's a sunny spring morning and my mother's making coffee. Eleanor is lovely to listen to with her Staten Island accent and chunky jewelry and her glamorous New York haircut that she says is called a "Fellini pageboy."

"You're supposed to wear really dark eye makeup, white lipstick, and be at least five foot seven, but I'm just doing the hair thing," she intones in a voice that is the height of sophistication.

Eleanor smokes constantly but never coughs like Aunt Maria and never has yellow fingers like Pa. She laughs easily and is always hugging me cuz she loves me and can't have a child of her own. My parents are going off to church. I'm not. I said I have a fever, even though I feel fine. Eleanor is staying home with me.

When my parents leave, Eleanor throws away my breakfast of soggy cereal and repulsive canned pears. She knows I want to be just like her when I grow up—free, pretty, and from New York—and that right now I want to play our special game which we can only do on the q.t. She quickly gets me a coffee cup and pours some coffee with a lot of milk and lets me spoon in the sugar myself. Then she gives me a cigarette. 'Course she doesn't light it—I am only ten and we've agreed that I can pretend to smoke until I'm old enough to move to New York, where every working girl gets up and has coffee and a cigarette first thing in the morning.

She grabs one of her shorter, filmy dressing gowns from her suitcase in the living room and puts it on me over my pajamas and then gets into one herself, even though she's already dressed.

We smoke, have more coffee, and chat about late trains, our boyfriends, when we'll get our nails done, and how much of our paychecks we'll spend on new shoes, know what I mean? We look out the kitchen window and see all those New York taxis speeding by. Eleanor suggests that we take one later on. Uptown. I think that's a great idea. Eleanor actually does most of the talking, but I always catch on pretty fast and join in as best as I can. We wonder if we'll go to the Waldorf this year for New Year's Eve. It's a difficult decision. You have to make reservations so far in advance.

Wouldn't you know my parents walk in just as I'm taking a particularly long drag from my cigarette, which my father grabs out of my mouth and rips into pieces, sending tobacco flying all over the place.

He screams at Eleanor, "Cigarettes kill you, you stupid bitch." He paces around the kitchen as he yells. "Everyone in your family gets lung cancer. Don't they ever think that smoking might have something to do with it?"

Actually that isn't exactly true. Many of our Staten Island relations did die of cancer, but a lot of the women had breast, not lung cancer.

"And who the hell do you think you are, risking Bridget's life by tempting her with these damn cancer sticks? She's just an innocent child. It's bad enough that she has to breathe in all of your damn cigarette smoke. But now you've got her pretending that she's smoking, herself?"

My father seems to know more about smoking than the Surgeon General.

Eleanor tries to make peace. "C'mon, Patrick. We're just having a little daydream. You can't blame people for dreaming, right?"

He stops pacing right by Eleanor's chair and towers over her, pointing his finger back and forth at her face. "Dreams? Daydreams? Pipe dreams, Eleanor. Stupid, foolish, pipe dreams. You people are all alike."

He shakes his head and starts to move away from her but then turns back and curses her: "I'm going to outlive you, you cheap guinea, by decades, because I stopped smoking once they said it was bad for you. But you, you and your pipe dreams, don't have the willpower to stop."

Then he turns to me. "And what do you have to say for yourself, missy? You planning on growing up to be trash like this?"

I wish he was pointing to the ashtray but know he's pointing at Eleanor. My father is calling Eleanor—my New York aunt who's free and single and has a Fellini pageboy—trash. She bites her bottom lip, hardens her face, lights another cigarette, and stares out the kitchen window. But somehow, even in her defiance, she looks smaller.

In that moment, I know he's gone too far. Eleanor and the Staten Island relatives will leave today. She and I might never play our game again.

"You wanna die young too?" he yells at me, spit gathering in the corners of his mouth.

I might never become a New York single working girl. I might not even ever get to see the Waldorf.

I stand up and slowly take off Eleanor's dressing gown and fold it over my chair. I look right at him and then over at Eleanor. What can I say?

"No," I mumble softly and walk toward my bedroom. I glance back but Eleanor just keeps smoking and staring out that kitchen window.

9. Staten Island Ladies of Cootras

"Aunt Louisa and Aunt Esther aren't technically your aunts," my mother explains. "Aunt Esther is Uncle A's cousin, and Louisa and Esther are something like half-sisters." It's hard to figure out everyone's exact relationship to everyone else with the Staten Island Italian relatives cuz there's so many of them.

My father shakes his head. "They aren't technically anything," he spits and storms out of the room, dismissing Aunts Louisa and Esther and the whole Staten Island family in one swift sentence.

I always want to hear more about any of the Staten Island relations since I have so few aunts, uncles, or cousins in Boston, and it's always a major event when they come to town. As well as my aunts, there's "Little Sophie" (I think she's one of my grandmother's cousin's nieces) and "Big Sophie" (my grandmother), and "Aunt E" and "Cousin E," an indeterminable number of Joes and Als, and Jildas in many shapes and sizes. Although I can't picture every one of them, I love to think of all of those people related to each other—and to me—doing things together out there on Staten Island.

Aunt Eleanor is, I'm sure, the most glamorous person on all of Staten Island. We call her once during the visit, and she sounds pretty even on the phone. But because of her new job on the twenty-third floor of a big office building, Eleanor'll hardly ever have time to visit us in Cambridge anymore. 'Course I know why she's really not coming. After that fight when my father cursed her, she might never stay with us again. I console myself by thinking of her wearing slim sheath dresses and high heels, clicking around the office every day, and pray she'll change her mind and take the train to surprise us all. Then she and I could play our game.

All that I relish about the Staten Island relatives drives my father nuts. A few come to visit in the spring, but the big trip is every July, when they arrive noisily with a trailer, which they set up in my grandparents' driveway. According to my father, vacationing in a trailer is just plain low class. Uncle G, a short and wiry man with a quick smile and elfin moves, puts down lawn chairs around the trailer so everyone who wants can sit and snack and drink in the sun. My father has to be in the shade because his fair Irish skin burns easily. About four o'clock every afternoon, when it's too hot for anyone else, I can find Uncle G in one of those lawn chairs with a steaming cup of coffee and a cigar.

"Never too hot for your old Uncle G," he proclaims one afternoon. "Because I have a clean conscience. The flames of hell are reserved for evildoers, and you can tell who they are because the heat bothers them."

I start making a mental list of people I know who can't stand hot weather—and then he winks at me to show he's kidding. My father hates jokes about religion.

I'm never allowed in their trailer, but I'm always curious about it. "It isn't much to look at," says Aunt E, Uncle G's wife, who has a gruff voice inside a tiny body. She strokes my hair as I hang around the door one day. "It gives us a place to sleep and lets us be able to see your Nana Sophie and Pa Joe whenever they want us."

"It's functional," says Uncle A, taking a long drag from his cigarette, the sun reflecting off his bald head. "And that's all we need."

But that isn't all Aunt Esther and Aunt Louisa need. They never sleep in the trailer. They stay in my grandparents' spare bedroom.

My father dislikes Esther and Louisa intensely. 'Course there's all the usual Irish-Italian conflict, with Italians, regardless of their money, status, or trailers, still somehow being "just off the boat." Which, when you think about it, is actually kind of true about people who live on Staten Island. But Esther and Louisa also have such unusual and not very Catholic-sounding beliefs about women, which I think is the main reason behind my father's loathing. They're always mentioning Greek myths and how women embody, embrace, and sustain the "life-force"—even though the two of them are pretty old.

Imagine how that goes over with my father—lead balloon, you know, and he doesn't keep his feelings on the q.t. They think men should worship us because we're "cyclical like the earth," and that the goddess Demeter is the mother of all mortals (and maybe immortals too) and the creator of the Earth. They even identify a little with Demeter and once in a while call me "our Persephone," which I love, but it makes my father say, "Demeter? Sounds more like Demented if you ask me." Not that anyone has.

Esther and Louisa, but particularly Louisa, are normally quite withdrawn. Esther's dark and larger boned. Louisa is frail, with thin, light-brown hair. Most of the Staten Island relations are quite old, but Esther and Louisa are a different kind of old. They're old ladies and this also may be why they don't sleep in the trailer. My mother says they're very devoted to each other, and if I had a sister, even a half-sister, I know we'd be devoted too.

A couple of summers ago, they began to educate me, as Louisa intoned softly, in "the finer things of female accoutrements." I was flattered, even though I'd never heard of "cootras." Everyone found my term hilarious and, much to my embarrassment, it stuck. But I try to be thick-skinned about it because Esther and Louisa's lessons are truly magnificent.

They've taught me about posture and hats, dignity and makeup, jewelry and gloves, and they've explained so many Greek myths, especially those about Aphrodite, Diana (whose other name is Artemis), Athena, and Gaea. Sometimes my friends get in on the Greek myths discussions, which they really enjoy. Esther and Louisa encourage us to put on plays about stories of goddesses and all their powers which we do in Agnes's backyard.

But now, in what Louisa says is "the important summer of my tenth year," our concentration is to be on perfumes and fabrics.

"You'll be wearing perfume soon, Bridget," Louisa reveals one morning, "and it's high time you develop an awareness of your scent preferences."

Scent preferences. I love the notion.

"Let's put this one on your left wrist," Louisa hums, energetically for her, "and see what you think."

The bottle is clear and round with a purple bulb at the top, which Louisa squeezes in the air near my hand.

It feels cool so I put my nose to my palm and sniff. My head reels. My eyes water. This is worse than window washing.

Louisa purses her lips. I'm not doing very well.

"It's kind of nice, but maybe it's not my preference." I'm trying to sound mature and appreciative and not to cough.

Louisa sighs. She reaches out her hand to Esther, who takes it and gives her a reassuring nod. "Get me the Arpège, would you, dear."

Louisa locks her eyes on mine. "Arpège is a romantic scent. It's been around since 1927, so it's got a history." With the confidence of what I see as a highly trained nose, she smells the bottle, which must have some perfume residue on it. "Oh, the honeysuckle and jasmine and that faint hint of orange blossoms." She looks rapturous.

"This is too old for you now," Louisa confides, "but it may still be more to your liking."

Arpège—a rich golden brown in a crystal bottle—must be a serious perfume. I start to worry because I'm sensitive to smells in general and prone to feeling rather nauseated in the presence of too much perfume. Doctor Whalen says my stomach is nervous and he's recently prescribed peppermint oil (rather than more of that revolting chocolate aspirin), which I now take whenever my parents fight and sometimes sneak when I've swallowed a bit of steak or roast beef. But I need to be strong for Aunt Louisa.

"Right wrist," Louisa says curtly. "Just a small spritz because it's very expensive."

I don't need to put my nose to my wrist—the odor overpowers me. This is the kind of perfume my mother and I smell if we sit too close to the younger, more attractive women in church. The kind that, if we arrived early, my mother says is enough to allow us to move pews, even though we might look rude. "Better than throwing up before the Kyrie," she whispers, and we both giggle and slip away to a pew that isn't near anyone looking fashionable. The older women in our parish usually smell of mothballs, which, while kind of stinky, doesn't give us headaches or upset stomachs.

So there I am, with a different scent on each wrist, hoping that someone will open a window. Louisa's against even raising the blinds, let alone the windows, and I'm never really sure why, but it seems she worries that the furniture, or even she herself, might fade in the presence of too much light.

"Enough for today," Louisa proclaims. "Wear these perfumes all day and inhale them from time to time. Tomorrow we can try some others."

I thank both my aunts and force myself not to rush from the room, trying to exit like a lady, even though I'm wearing sneakers, a tee shirt, and seersucker shorts, and feel like I could barf. Once the door closes, I make a beeline for the bathroom and scrub and scrub, on the q.t. of course, with the special soap my grandfather keeps in a bucket under the sink for washing off paint or grease from working around the house.

Even though I'm lightheaded, I'm so pleased my aunts think I'm old enough to develop my scent preferences. It's obvious that they could never stay in the trailer because womanhood like theirs takes up a lot of space. One has to set out those perfume bottles just so on a wooden dresser with a nice dresser scarf underneath, and no matter what the trailer's like inside, there can't be room for dressers with scarves.

In addition to scents, this summer I'm learning about fabrics, and Louisa's decided to focus on silk. One morning I'm invited in before they've even finished dressing and cleaning up the room, though it's fairly late. "The heat makes us all so slow-moving," Esther calls out to me from a half-open door, "so we aren't quite ready for you, but if we don't start now, we'll never get your silk cootras in before lunch." Louisa scowls at her. She doesn't approve of ladies making verbal errors because "it shows poorly on their social class." Esther finds it all amusing and smiles, pulling gently on my braids.

After a quick good-morning hug, Louisa starts immediately. "Silk was first woven in the eighth century." She lowers her voice so she sounds like the narrator on those Mutual of Omaha wildlife programs. Still in her lace-trimmed, sleeveless violet nightgown, which exposes the wrinkly flesh on her thin upper arms, she rummages through the closet to find something "cool enough to wear." I think her freshly manicured, rose-beige nails are quite glamorous, even if she has at least two dozen age spots on her hands. I follow her around the small room as she picks up a tortoise-shell comb for her thin hair, lifts her stockings out of the top drawer of the bureau, and lays out her undergarments—girdle, bra, and full slip—at the bottom of the bed and then, finally, a dress. She's decided on her yellow cotton print, three-quarter-length-sleeve dress. Esther grabs my shoulders from behind and tells me to sit down on the side of the bed, which is still unmade, cuz there isn't space for three of us to walk around their bedroom.

Louisa stops momentarily and looks off into the distance—at least as much as a person can in a bedroom with the blinds down and a window that faces the neighbor's house—then smiles with relish. "Silkworms eat only mulberry leaves—imagine that—just one special food for all of the creatures that help us make such a beautiful fabric. And they eat thousands of pounds of them, not knowing what their fate is about to be."

She pauses to see if I know what that fate is and takes off her nightgown, having managed to put on all her underwear and her full slip underneath it, then steps into her dress. Esther helps her zip it up and, following a quick head nod of Louisa's, finds some pearls and hooks them around Louisa's thin neck. Sensing my ignorance, Louisa leans forward, so close that I can smell her mouthwash. "If they let the silkworms come out of their cocoons themselves, they'd make holes in the silk thread. So they have to be baked to death and then boiled."

I gasp.

Despite being a lady, Louisa seems to enjoy the look of my grim, blinking expression.

Then, as if on cue, a garment bag Esther has taken silently from the closet falls to the floor, and together Esther and Louisa hold out a deep-red dress made of silk crepe. "It takes about two thousand cocoons to make this dress," Louisa declares proudly. "In Japan." She lightly touches the folds with her fingertips and leans into me. "Look at the way it drapes." Her soft voice is back. "Clean your hands and you can touch it. But dry them carefully."

Esther has a wet facecloth ready and assures Louisa this is enough, so long as I dry my hands on another cloth she produces from her pocket. Finally I'm allowed to run my fingers over what I think is an unusual, rather fleshy texture. I've never touched silk crepe before, and it gives me an odd sensation inside myself, know what I mean?

Louisa and Esther look at me expectantly. I see I'm required to say something after such an intense discussion and dramatic display. I touch the dress again, and there's that sensation again. It's like the one I sometimes get when I read about the virgin martyrs.

Suddenly I imagine Mary Magdalene, "the apostle to the apostles," wearing a gown of red silk crepe after her seven devils have been exorcized, and all the apostles can't stop glancing at her.

And Jesus turns to her.

And I am Mary Magdalene.

And Jesus and the twelve apostles watch me as I gently smooth one of the folds of my red silk crepe garment, and I can see they want to know what it's like to touch that undulating fabric, and what I feel like when I stroke it.

Aunt Esther sneezes quite loudly. What am I doing? I've certainly never had thoughts like this about any of the fabrics my mother and I sew with. Cotton. Seersucker. Wool. I don't think Mary Magdalene would have worn clothes made of those materials.

They're both waiting.

My hands are getting sweaty, so I move them away from the dress and take a deep breath.

"Fabrics from both Japan and Staten Island are very complex," I assert in my most serious, grown-up voice, and their smiles tell me I've said the right thing. At least I manage to keep Mary Magdalene and the apostles on the q.t.

Many of Louisa and Esther's blouses and skirts are silk—of varying colors and weights—a few of the lightest chiffon. Some are covered with little tucks and others have unusual buttonholes or self-made tiny silk rosette buttons. We admire their craftsmanship as Esther brings one after another out of the closet, each in its own cloth garment bag.

Then Louisa looks at me with slightly teary eyes. "Remember the silkworms, cara mia. Life can be like that, and you'll see, even in the move into your own womanhood, that you'll require things for the transition—the way the silkworms crave the mulberry leaves—that you won't need or want after you've made it."

Does Louisa mean I need her now but won't later? That'll never happen. But whatever she's trying to say, I decide right then that I'll wear nothing but silk when I'm a woman. Even in the summer, despite the heat. Even in the winter, despite the cold. Despite the worms' fate. Even more than Louisa wears it. Or Mary Magdalene. I imagine myself dressing slowly in front of a mirror in matching ivory and not Mary Magdalene red, but Virgin Mary blue silk clothing. Everything is silk, from my bra and panties, to my slip, to my lovely blue and ivory flared dress. A halter dress. Maybe there are tiny bits of red on the bra and panties.

My father's always invited for dinner at Nana and Pa's one night when the Staten Island relatives are visiting. 'Course, unsurprisingly, this leads to the same argument every year.

"I'm too busy to come."

And the fight begins. I stay until my mother starts to cry. Then I slip out the back door, down the two flights of stairs, and walk along to my best friend Agnes's apartment.

Two of my other friends, Donna and Lucy, are there. When I arrive they're in Agnes's room playing Fallen Saint Stories. At ten years old, we're all starting to think a lot more about sex but are still too nervous to talk about it directly. So our game has evolved—we still speculate on sins involving sex from our Bible Stories and Saints books, but now we compare them, whenever relevant, to people we know, especially older boys in the neighborhood.

This afternoon they've been rereading Mary Magdalene stories and talking about what exactly sins of the flesh could actually entail. Lucy informs me that I missed some juicy stuff about Robbie O'Donnell and Nina Jones, which she promises to fill me in on later. Donna and Agnes are wondering how hard it would be to show humility and repentance by washing a person's feet. They make room for me to come and sit on the floor and ask what I think.

Quickly we all agree that one of our sins would have to be pretty bad to get us to wash someone's feet—especially if the feet were really dirty and shampoo hadn't been invented yet. But the thought of the sin part is still kind of exciting.

"Oh, c'mon," Donna says, "let's try." I'm dwelling too much on my parents fighting and want something to distract me. "Let's do it," I say. "We can imagine something sinful we've done—or might do—and then wash each other's feet and see if we feel atoned," I suggest with more enthusiasm than I feel.

With her usual flair for drama, Lucy works out our role-playing so that we'll preserve the Biblical feeling necessary to keep us from any sinful paths of our own. We all have long hair and can take turns playing Mary Magdalene and Jesus, pretending to wash each other's feet. Our hair will stay dry, of course, and we'll put on clean socks, which Agnes pulls out of her top drawer. We don't care if they match or not.

Agnes and I and Donna and Lucy are partners. Agnes sits in her chair while I unbraid my hair, and Donna pulls hers out of her ponytail. Donna and I will be Mary Magdalenes first. I begin to think about Robbie and sins I could commit with him and bend my head over Agnes's feet, saying, "Oh Robbie" very softly. I rub my hair all over the yellow sock on Agnes's left foot and the white sock on her right. Then we change places and she says she'll think about Michael Lehy while she washes my feet.

Agnes and I are pretty hysterical and congratulating ourselves on the new variation we've made up when Lucy screams to Donna, "Get away, you lezzy!"

Donna seems to have gotten carried away with her role as Mary Magdalene and started to move up Lucy's legs with her hair—washing them on the inside and well above the knee. "This game sucks and Donna, you're queer," Lucy cries. Then she looks at her watch and says she's late for dinner anyway and quickly leaves.

Donna shrugs off Lucy's accusations. "Just shows how desperate she is."

Agnes is ready to discuss whether we're feeling any sense of atonement for our sins or humility from our foot-washing experiences, but Lucy's yelling reminded me of my parents, and I decide I should leave to see how it's going. Donna needs to get home too.

"That Mary Magdalene was a real slut, huh?" she asks me as we walk down the stairs.

The next afternoon, when we're waiting for my father to come for dinner, I look for Louisa and Esther, but Louisa has hung her "Do Not Disturb. Thank you. The Waldorf" sign on the door. She often needs to take a sponge bath and rest on hot afternoons.

"Wash your hands, Bridget, and come help us in the kitchen. There's still a lot to do," calls one of my aunts, who must have noticed me hanging around Esther and Louisa's door. Sometimes it seems that grown-ups feel that whenever anything is wrong, it can be solved by asking me to wash my hands.

When my father finally arrives, things really tense up. Somehow he manages to convey, without saying much of anything, that he's been at work all day, which they haven't; that he's driven in hot traffic, which they haven't; and that he's tired and wants to come home to the peace and quiet of his own apartment and not to a lot of cackling Italians who drink too much wine and eat too much garlic.

My mother looks frightened for most of the evening. "I'll stay behind to help clean up," she says with a stiff smile on her face, clearly upset and wanting to make amends.

So my father and I set off walking home. I begin to tell him about Aunt Louisa and Aunt Esther and their cootras and how this year more than ever I can see that they are real Staten Island ladies and how important it is for me to consider clothing and scent preferences. My father usually likes it when I tell him stories, but he stops dead on the sidewalk and glares at me, his face crimson and stern. "Bridget, I can't bear another word about Louisa and Esther and the ladies of Staten Island and scent preferences. Those two old cats. Ladies of the evening, more like it."

I don't know how exactly I take in the meaning of "ladies of the evening," but it reminds me of sins of the flesh and Mary Magdalene, only it isn't titillating like when Agnes and I washed each other's feet.

I fall asleep before my mother gets home, wondering if my aunts really are "ladies of the evening" rather than Demeters and if my mother knows and if everyone knows and if I'm low class and if garlic really doesn't taste good and whether it's shameful for men to have jobs where their hands get dirty and if Nana drinks too much. I try not to think about being half-Italian. And I don't want to imagine my womanhood coming on.

After that night, I want the Staten Island relations to go home. I sit sullenly in the living room while my grandfather chain-smokes and talks to my aunts and uncles, laughing and eating and sipping lemonade. My mother watches me and finally announces that she and I are going for a walk. Once outside, she scolds me for my moodiness.

"Why do you think Esther and Louisa have brought all those clothes with them?" she whispers, rushing us around the corner from my grandparents'. I don't say anything.

"Surely not to wear in the hot summer." Then she stops and grabs my shoulders. "They've brought them to show you because you're the youngest girl in the family. They have no daughters and they love you so much. Why d'you think they have so many clothes and know so much about fabrics?" Her eyes burn into mine.

I pull away. What if she knows? And she's going to tell me? I can't stand to hear it again. "I don't know," I scream right there on the street. "And I don't want to know. Don't tell me." I start to run but she catches my arm.

"They worked for years together in the garment district," she shouts. "Hard, long hours. In fact, that's how they met."

We must look like a couple of nutcases to anyone on the street, yelling and pulling at each other.

"Years ago...are you listening, Bridget?" she says over the traffic. "Louisa wasn't a fast seamstress, and Esther helped her out." She reaches for my hand as we cross at a busy intersection. "And then they finally left because Louisa wasn't well and she hated working in a factory, and they started a small shop of their own on Staten Island in a house that Uncle A, who was very understanding when you think about it, bought for them, and they lived together above the shop."

She's hurling words at me, the way she talks when she and my father fight. Why are both my parents all of a sudden so interested in telling me family secrets about the Staten Island relatives?

"Truth be told, Esther did most of the sewing, but Louisa could usually convince customers to buy a more expensive fabric than they'd come in for. And Esther was happy for them just to be together and not have the commute." My mother pauses to laugh, which relaxes me a bit. "Can't you picture Louisa telling someone who wanted Esther to make them a nice cotton dress that they'd look much more elegant in a silk kimono and managing to persuade them?"

I don't know what to think. Is my mother making all this up to hide things from me? Does she really not know? Can this be the truth? For all of my life, they've just been my aunts. Then they became...I force myself to think the word...prostitutes... which feels terrible and really wrong, especially when they seem more like older goddesses. Now they're dressmakers. "They never talked to me about working," I say, holding on to my father's account of them.

"Well, how do you think they can afford to have all those clothes?" she asks.

"How many men came as customers?" I say, sounding like my father and still hearing his voice. I'm angry and ashamed that I even associate with women like this, that my mother doesn't know what's been going on, that I have to live with endless family secrets, and in a world where women certainly aren't the life-force.

"What an odd question." My mother looks askance at me. "I suppose a few men, from time to time, would ask them to make a hat or a dress for their wives or sweethearts for Easter or a birthday, but probably only if the woman was a regular customer and Esther had the measurements on hand. She never liked doing alterations."

I look up at the cloudless sky that says everyone should be enjoying a day like this and wonder why I'm finding it so hard to believe that my mother's telling me the truth, since everything she says makes sense, redeems the Staten Island relatives whom I love, Esther and Louisa who, face it, I adore, and my mother herself, still the center of my universe. But I can't rid myself of my father's words. We walk the rest of the way in silence.

When we get back to Nana and Pa's, I feel a little better, and Esther has a small present wrapped up for me. "Open it now, while we're all here," she says, giving me a tentative hug. "I want to see how you like it."

It's a lovely small cameo with a black background and a white bust of a woman carved on it that looks like icing sugar but is rock hard. Louisa explains that the chain is made of delicate white gold to match the tiny white-gold filigree encircling the cameo.

Esther asks me to treat the box gently because she was given this cameo as a young girl. In this very box. It came all the way from Italy, and the jeweler's name is still on the outside. Inside, she's written a short inscription in a shaky hand. Even though I can't read it, I thank her and start to sob.

"The cameo. It's Persephone," says Esther.

"That's you," Louisa smiles at me.

"From your two Demeters. You remember from our last visit, don't you?"

I nod my head and begin crying again. My mother fastens the cameo around my neck. I turn to hug her tightly because I know that everything she told me about my Demeters must be true.

And Esther says, "Surely the poor girl's hormones are coming in," and Louisa starts on some speech about hormones, but nobody seems to be listening.

After I calm down and am sitting with everyone in the living room, I begin wondering how the cameo would look with that blue and ivory silk flared halter dress with the matching panties and bra underneath that have small flecks of red, and whether I should wear my hair loose or pulled back, when I noticed that Aunt Louisa and Aunt Esther aren't sitting with us.

I rush into their room but they aren't there. I check the kitchen and the bathroom but can't find them. I run outside into the backyard around to the driveway, and then I spot them, just inside the door of the trailer. Louisa's head is on Esther's shoulder, her arm around Esther's waist. Esther's hand is gently touching the inside of Louisa's leg, above the knee.

I stop running and stare at them. My head spins with images. Mary Magdalene. Sins of the flesh. Donna's hair. Lucy's leg. "Get away!" Ladies of the evening.

Esther sees me first. She and Louisa slowly separate and look at me. I can hear my parents' voices as my heart pounds in my ears. "They live together above the shop." "Devoted to each other." "They aren't technically your aunts." "They aren't technically anything."

I want to scream out, "They are technically something. They are my aunts. They are dressmakers. They came into their womanhood a long time ago. They are my Demeters. And they are Our Staten Island Ladies of Cootras."

But this is not a time for screaming. I touch the cameo around my neck and take a deep breath, willing myself into ladylike behavior. I'm wearing my blue and ivory silk dress, now with matching pumps, and I have Arpège on my wrists and behind my ears. My hair is pulled back with a stunning silver clip. I walk slowly over to them, raising my head, and swallow hard.

"It's getting pretty smoky inside because Pa's handed out cigars, so I thought I'd come out here and be with you," I say quietly.

We look at each other, and no one speaks for a few moments.

"Want a tour of the trailer?" asks Louisa.

Esther holds the door open and I step inside.

10. The Bible, The Beatles, and Bubble Gum

Who would have thought the A&P would play such a crucial role in my spiritual development? This summer they're starting a campaign so that every Catholic family can afford a Bible. You just have to buy a thin, numbered box every week. One half-inch of Bible pages at a time. My mother and I get the first box for only twenty-nine cents. Twenty-nine cents! Almost as cheap as my missal from our Green Stamps. Which also came from the A&P.

The "installment Bible pamphlet" in Box Number One explains that the opening Bible pages are "genuine reproductions" of an illuminated manuscript. The kind that monks made by hand before there were printing presses. Just like the Spiritual Bouquets! The Bible also has many full-size religious pictures, mainly painted by Italians. That'll please my mother. Though it may annoy my father.

"It's a stupid come-on meant for gullible people like you two," my father shouts at my mother and me when he comes home from work to find us engrossed in the Bible pages, Box One, that we've laid out on the dining room table. My mother lost track of time and forgot to start dinner. Well, the Bible'll do that to you, won't it? I mean it's the Word of God, and even my father should see that the Bible is a lot more important than serving the pot roast on time. But he doesn't.

They get so angry about whether we can buy the other Bible boxes that eventually my mother throws a knife and then a fork at him. I'm starting to wonder if most people's parents hurl things at each other and everyone just keeps it on the q.t. Thank God she misses. But the knife is stuck in the wall.

"You'd try the patience of a saint!" my mother screams at him in one of her many saint-infused accusations. "We're talking about buying a Bible, not something frivolous!"

She is right about how difficult my father is. I just wish knives and forks didn't have to be involved. Eventually, of course, he has to give in. Even though the other installments cost $2.00 a box.

Though I'm keeping this on the q.t., reading the Bible has been such a disappointment. My overall impression, perhaps cuz I'm now eleven and a bit of a women's libber, is that God-the-F (as I'm now starting to call Him) has some pretty strange and sexist attitudes about females and that, really, He's so much worse than my father. Even.

I thought I knew the Adam and Eve story pretty well, but when you read it in the actual Bible as opposed to learning about it in school, it's really terrible for girls. God puts most of the blame for the fall on Eve. And His plan is to keep punishing married women throughout the ages and for all eternity: "To the woman he said, 'I will make great your distress in childbearing; in pain you shall bring forth children; for your husband shall be your longing, though he have dominion over you.'"

Why should it be painful to have children? That seems really unfair on women. Especially after they've been pregnant for nine months—and I've certainly heard mixed reviews about that experience. I'm well aware the Catholic Church believes in big families cuz every year in school I meet a new nun who can't believe I'm an only child. Sometimes they ask if I'm looking forward to a new little brother or sister. And one even assumed my mother was dead.

Now I'm wondering if maybe my parents have only me because childbirth and definitely pregnancy was so "greatly distressing" for my mother. She's told me many times that she threw up every single day for the whole nine months she was pregnant with me. Then she was in excruciating labor for over twenty-four hours before I finally arrived. I used to blame myself and felt really guilty for causing her pain before I was even born.

But now I realize it was all God-the-F having dominion over her just because she was a married woman trying to continue the human race. And I don't mean like Lot and his daughters, a story that my mother made me skip over quickly when it arrived in the third installment, even though I snuck back and looked. They actually made their father drunk and then "lay with him" (eew, imagine doing it with my father!) because the whole human race was going to die out if he didn't produce children.

A year ago I wouldn't have quite understood what that meant or believed it could be true, but I definitely do now. In my opinion, and if you can believe the Bible, God makes some pretty weird things happen. Especially to women, know what I mean? And He decided that husbands should always have the upper hand. How does that even make sense? They're at work all day and usually don't have a clue about what's going on at home. So why should they rule the roost? Why is God so cruel to women when Adam ate those apples too?

While my mother's ironing my father's shirts, I wonder whether I should talk to her about God's sexism, especially cuz she's still pretty mad at him about the Bible fuss. She turns away from the ironing board and switches the dial on the kitchen radio. Every station seems to be playing a Beatles song. "Damn it!" she says under her breath and turns the radio off.

I grab my transistor and plug in the earpiece so my mother can't hear it and catch the last half of "She Loves You." I tap my foot to the music. My mother glares at me, then hangs the third of my father's shirts on a clothesline she sometimes puts up in the kitchen. It looks like she has about a thousand more shirts to go. She sprinkles the next one with that special homemade starch—no spray starch for her—stares at the ironing pile, and sighs. I think that pile has dominion over my mother. This isn't the right time to ask her about God's feelings toward women.

I'm at the kitchen table, finishing a pop art poster in bright orange and yellow with a giant LOVE in the middle. I have another one just like it in blue and turquoise, except that it says PEACE. Lately, I've been babysitting for the British family across the street, the Ellises. Whenever the little girl doesn't get her own way, she runs up to the attic to scratch her mosquito bites and comes down bleeding all over her incredibly translucent skin, which is too stigmata-like to be believed. And she's not even Catholic.

I don't like babysitting for her, but her brother's all right and the mother's totally cool. Mrs. Ellis is the one who taught me about sexism. She's a pop artist and makes posters for local events, like if someone is giving a speech in Harvard Square against the war. She also loves my artwork.

"Bridey, you make the best fat and curly pop art letters I've ever seen," she told me a few weeks ago. Maybe I can ask Mrs. Ellis about God. She's having me create some pages with this special geometric shaping and coloring that's her "signature style," and she's adding my pages to her portfolio cuz when she gets her next job, she might use something of mine. Then I could get paid for my art.

My mother's finished ironing another shirt. I'm coloring in the V. Mrs. Ellis says my mother shouldn't iron, that it's against women's lib. Mrs. Ellis is a real women's libber, which means that her husband has wrinkled shirts and their apartment is a total mess unless I do some housework on the q.t. while I'm babysitting. It just about drove my mother through the roof when she found out I was cleaning for the Ellises.

"She hardly pays you anything as it is, Bridget, and if you wash her dirty bathtub one more time, you can kiss that babysitting job good-bye and come home and do household chores here."

I told Mrs. Ellis that we had to lay off the cleaning cuz I definitely want to keep working for her, and she said it was okay and that I "deserved a little liberation too." Then she asked me to work for them all day on Sunday, but when I told her I had to go to church first, she rolled her eyes. I probably shouldn't ask Mrs. Ellis about God either.

I don't fully understand what women's lib is, and at first I thought it was just a British thing. But now I've discovered, from comments my father makes when he's reading the *Globe*, that there's a women's lib movement starting in our country too. Last night he really exploded. "Next they'll be having men wearing aprons and doing the cooking like that fairy, John, from the beauty parlor."

When I said that Mr. Ellis made a lot of their dinners and that I thought it was a good idea for husbands to cook, my father got really mean. "Listen, missy, don't hold your breath about getting paid for one of those posters you're always making.

Mrs. Ellis would do well to cook more and get her head out of her artsy clouds. I'm sure she isn't paid for most of her jobs. Which is why you only get seventy-five cents an hour to watch her kids while everyone else in the whole of Cambridge earns a dollar an hour."

When I looked shocked that my father knew about my posters and the going rate for babysitting, he snapped at me again. "Yeah, I've heard all about the cleaning too. We're trying to protect you from spongers like them. She's paying you in dreams."

I'm definitely not asking my father.

Women's lib makes me kind of nervous cuz from what I do understand, it definitely isn't supposed to be for Catholics. I really paid attention this year when we studied Adam and Eve and the Fall from Paradise again. If you think about women's lib, you notice that God's strange attitudes were present from the beginning of time. He made Adam first and then Eve from Adam's rib. So right away she's second-rate. He didn't have to create Eve like that. He could have spun her out of thin air. Or dramatically made a star fall and turned it into her. Because He's God and can do anything. So He must have wanted her to seem inferior. I never thought like this before I knew Mrs. Ellis.

Our religion textbook says that Adam wasn't deceived by Satan, that Eve is the only one who's sinful. But that's not true. Adam knew those apples weren't supposed to be eaten, so why didn't he say something? I think Adam is what Mrs. Ellis terms a "spineless git," which she called her husband the other day when he didn't want to talk to their landlord about something.

So while poor Eve was being driven crazy by that talking snake—something I can totally empathize with—and decided to ask Adam about the apples, she probably simply wanted a healthy debate. But no. Not from pathetic git Adam.

Mr. Ellis is an important doctor, so I don't suppose he really is a spineless git like Adam at all. But ever since he said he had to examine my breasts to check if I needed a bra and then asked me to keep it on the q.t., I feel a little uncomfortable with him. Especially since Mrs. Ellis says that women's libbers aren't supposed to wear bras. There's no way I can ask Mr. Ellis.

My only choice is my best friend, Agnes. We can talk about anything, even though she's not that into religion anymore. When I go over to her place, Agnes is in her bedroom, reading a book that she quickly shoves behind her bed when she sees me.

"Well, do you get what a virgin is? I mean hymen and the whole nine yards. And how exactly you lose it?"

"Yes, Ag, I most certainly do," I say, trying to sound like I've always known, even though virginity isn't what I want to be talking about.

She narrows her eyes. "How'd you find out?"

Well, I'm not about to explain that losing your virginity has absolutely nothing to do with riding a bike. Really, when you think about it, what kind of bizarre bicycle seat shapes did my father have in mind? I don't want to think about it. That whole bike fight story is definitely on the q.t. Last year, though, when I was wondering how the Virgin Mary could be a virgin and a mother, I found library books with full anatomy lessons, even colored plates. So I understand exactly how a female gets pregnant and has a baby, but Mary having Jesus and still being a virgin? It's pretty difficult to understand. Or believe. I guess that's what a miracle is.

"I'll bet it was a book," says Agnes. "But never mind. Just describe it to me, so I can see if you really understand it all."

So I tell her. Her eyes grow wide at parts of my explanation and she nods at others. We both agree that "it" seems totally disgusting. I decide to keep my theory about God-the-F's attitude on the q.t. right at the moment cuz even if Agnes thinks I got my information from a book, I don't want her imagining that religion had anything to do with it.

Agnes opens her top dresser drawer and takes out one of those big, turquoise, bubble-gum cigars we both love. She puts a bunch of Beatles singles on her record player with that special drop-down adaptor for 45s. She's so lucky to have a record player right in her room. She peels the cellophane off the cigar, and we each bite off a chunk. We stop talking for a few moments to get the gum mashed down in our mouths and start chewing in rhythm to "Love Me Do." My mother never lets me have this kind of gum because she says it'll rot your teeth.

"D'ya think the others know?" Agnes asks. She means Donna, Lucy, and Anne.

"I think they get the general stuff, but not the specifics.

Agnes beams at me. "Well then, Bridey, aren't we just so clever?"

"Yup," I smile, thinking how innocent Agnes is about all God has in store for us when we get married and lose our virginity. This seems to be the best time to ask her. "Agnes, I was wondering what you thought about the Adam and Eve story and why you think God-the-Father is so mean to Eve and, really, to all women?" I play it pretty cool by not mentioning the Bible and swaying with my eyes kind of closed to "I Want to Hold Your Hand."

"This gum is making me really thirsty," says Ag, who goes to the kitchen to get us some grape Kool-

Aid, but reminds me not to drink it for a few minutes cuz it washes away part of the delicious gum taste. I'm waiting for her to say she couldn't care less about Adam and Eve, but the book she's reading on the q.t. also has an Adam in it. So she actually really wants to talk about them. Another case of God working in strange ways.

"I can't imagine they've all totally missed the point of the whole Paradise story," says Agnes. Then she shakes her head. "Nah, they aren't telling us because they think we're too young."

"Too young for what?"

Agnes rolls her eyes at me. "Virginity, Bridget? You can yak on and on about it but does it really sink in with you?"

I can't see what Agnes is getting at, so I just sing along with the Beatles, thinking about feeling happy and being touched inside. Inside what?

"Oh, come on," says Agnes. "It's obviously not apples that upset God so much."

"Maybe not," I say. I'm certainly capable of reading symbolically. "The apples could've been pears or oranges or anything He didn't want them to do, like not drinking water out of a certain spring. The point is He said something was forbidden, and they disobeyed Him by doing it anyway."

"No," laughs Agnes. "Every kid is told that Adam and Eve's real sin was disobedience. But it wasn't. They only say that because they're trying to teach us to obey."

Agnes gets off the bed to turn up the record player. The Beatles are the most amazing four guys in the universe. Everyone's in love with Paul, and 'course I am too, but I'd really be happy with just George.

"It's all about sex, Bridey," Agnes smiles, dancing back to the bed and singing, "when will you understand?" She then gives a dramatic pause. "And virginity!"

"What are you talking about, Agnes? There's no sex in the Garden of Eden. It's a holy place," I shout over the song. Agnes dances back to turn down the volume. Lately she finds sex in everything.

"The Bible writers used 'apples' to be polite, but they really meant something else." Agnes sounds so superior. Even though we're both eleven, you'd think she was years older.

"Bridget, everyone but kids are clued into what the expulsion from Paradise really means." Agnes opens a drawer and pulls out her missal. "Here's a really big hint." She tries to sound like Ed Sullivan.

Taking a sip of Kool-Aid, Agnes moves to the middle of her room and turns to a page in her missal with a piece of yarn in it. She clears her throat. "O Lord, open my lips and I shall praise your name." Agnes smiles at me.

I shake my head. I'm still clueless.

Agnes looks at me and sighs. "Prepare yourself. God-the-Father had a thing for Eve. He wanted her to 'open her lips to Him' in order to 'praise his name.' So to speak," and Agnes rolls on the bed, laughing. Then we both finally take big swigs of our Kool-Aid.

I see. Agnes isn't referring to the lips on your face, know what I mean? She's talking about the other ones. The ones near your virginity.

"But Eve wasn't interested in God-the-Father, was she?" Agnes smiles. "She liked a totally different apple. Adam. And she wanted to be Adam's apple. That's what 'Adam's apple' really means." I thought an Adam's apple was something in your throat. But I'm not about to interrupt Agnes. "And Satan told her to go for it. So she did! She opened her lips to Adam even though God-the-Father wanted her for Himself."

I can't believe that the whole Paradise story could actually be about boyfriends and having sex.

"I get it because it's just like what happens in this book I'm reading."

"Agnes, stop!" I shout. "You're being sacrilegious and God'll punish you."

Agnes laughs at me so hard she suddenly has to pee. "That's the beauty of reading symbolically," she calls out as she runs to the bathroom. Agnes can be so annoying. In school I'm the one, not Agnes, who's really good at reading for hidden meaning.

"C'mon, just think about it, Bridey," Agnes yells from the hallway, running in, still pulling her pants up. "God-the-Father had the hots for Eve. And when He said, 'Don't eat the apples,' He clearly meant 'Don't touch the goods,'" she giggles. "That's the way my book puts it, anyway." I take another bite of the bubble gum cigar, trying to look blasé. Agnes is really on a roll.

"But Adam and Eve must've been wild for each other, regardless of what God said. That's why Satan could convince her. And why Adam jumped at Eve's offer."

I'm about to say I always thought Adam was a spineless git. But Agnes doesn't give me a chance.

"It's exactly the way Adam and Nina are in my book." She beckons for me to hand over the bubble gum cigar so she can gnaw off another chunk. We're going to use up the whole thing between the two of us. My jaws're getting tired but I'm not stopping. This is the biggest piece of gum I've ever had in my mouth.

Agnes reaches behind her bed for the book and hands it to me. *My Passion, My Innocence*. On the cover there's a big-breasted, young, blonde girl in a blue, low-cut dress, leaning back into the arms of an older-looking man with dark wavy hair with a touch of grey. "That's Nina and Adam," Ag says, like she's introducing me to real people. "It's my mother's book, if you can believe it! I found it hidden in her knitting basket. Turns out she's got a whole stash of them in the bottom cupboard of the pantry." She starts to read the back cover aloud. "A moving story of star-crossed lovers, longing to be together but forced apart by destiny."

Then Agnes lies back and starts to laugh so hard that she gags on her gum. She reaches for her Kool-Aid, and drinks it all. "Guess what I didn't want to tell you, Bridget?" And she starts laughing again. "I learned what exactly virginity is from a book! From this book! Isn't that so funny?"

I'm certain that the only thing my mother has in her knitting basket is yarn and knitting needles, and definitely nothing about virginity or star-crossed lovers. It's hard to imagine your mother even being aware of virginity, but 'course she must be.

"At any rate," says Ag, leafing through the book for some line, "if you catch on about Adam and Eve, maybe I'll let you borrow this. Okay?"

"Okay, thanks, Ag, though my parents'd die if they found a book with a cover like that in my room."

Agnes shrugs. "So even though Adam and Nina aren't meant to be together, they can't keep their hands off each other. Nina is supposed to marry Ned but falls in love with Adam. And her best friend tells her that loving Adam will be the worst because she'll be caught in a 'love triangle.' And we all know that everyone gets hurt in a love triangle."

I've never even heard of a love triangle, but I get it. Right away. Maybe Agnes is rubbing off on me.

"It must have been the same with Adam and Eve and God. Another love triangle," Agnes continues. She blows a huge bubble and pops it with her finger.

I think I can see where she's going with this.

"And He never fully got over it. He became filled with jealousy and spite, just like Ned. That's why He overreacted to the whole situation and evicted them from Paradise."

Agnes has so much flair. I feel pretty upset to think that God could suffer from the sin of Jealousy. But her ideas do explain a lot of His sexism against women. I can't wait to tell Mrs. Ellis. A love triangle. How could Agnes be clever enough to come up with all this? It really is a great symbolic reading.

"Yeah, totally," I say, taking more gum. "Adam was just as sinful as Eve. But cuz God was interested in Eve, she's the one He got furious with. And He's still angry with women, all cuz he lost Eve."

"Exactly!" Agnes says and pats me on the back. "Blaming Eve was a total cop-out, because, after all, it takes two to tango."

"But wait, Ag." I say suddenly. "I forgot. He's all-knowing, so we must be wrong."

"Nah," Agnes shakes her head, "love is blind."

Walking home from Agnes's, kicking the sneezy-fragrant fall leaves, my head pounds thinking how everyone gets hurt in a love triangle. Agnes is right about Adam and Eve and that vengeful God-the-F who still punishes women today for marrying men who aren't Him. And He's so sneaky. Getting men to do His dirty work. All those Bible lines about "submission" to your husbands. That's part of the punishment, because once you "open your lips" to someone other than Him, He sees you as a sinful, deceitful Eve.

So it's a love-triangle punishment that He inflicts on all married women. Over and over. "I will put enmity between you [that's the husband] and the woman, between your seed and her seed; he shall crush your head [that's the wife], and you shall lie in wait for his heel." God-the-F actually wants marriages to turn out badly. For someone who's part of a trinity, he sure hates triangles.

Once you accept that He wants "enmity" between husbands and wives, it does sort of explain why my mother and her sisters and my father's sister, and all my friends' mothers, including Agnes's, are pretty unhappy in their marriages. And what about "He shall crush your head"? That seems to encourage the kind of wife abuse Aunt Maria gets from Uncle Lou when he beats her up. All because He's imagining that every woman chose her husband and rejected Him. Control freak, know what I mean?

I walk into our yard and can hear my father shouting from our apartment. And that's Aunt Anna's voice. What's she doing here? And my mother's screaming. I run upstairs. Then stop and hide on the landing. My father's just dumped a whole bottle of garlic powder right down the sink. Anna regularly smuggles garlic to my mother, but I guess this time he caught them. He's running hot water and pushing them both over the sink to "smell the stench." He doesn't realize he actually likes food better when it has garlic in it. My mother's done taste tests on the q.t. 'Course she can't tell him. But there's always garlic hidden somewhere in our apartment.

"Let go, Patrick!"

"Stop it!"

"You son of a bitch...as bad as Mike."

It's Italians versus the Irish all over again, but how can people get so worked up about a spice?

As I watch my father with my mother and Aunt Anna, I decide that I'm not going to put up with this kind of crap from any man. Maybe I have to become a nun. Actually being a nun is a solid career option for a female these days, and I think a lot of married women would rather turn into pillars of salt than wake up for another day stuck with their husbands.

But when I run back to tell Agnes, she thinks I'm a nut case and says that my love of playing Barbies is evidence that I absolutely do not have a vocation.

"Be real! The nuns probably had visions when they were younger, like all those insane mystics in that book of yours who eat lepers' pus and their cats' vomit." Then Agnes reminds me how much more I started liking playing Barbies once she got a Ken doll. "Face it, Bridget, you 'can't help yourself.'" She's listening to the Four Tops and sings along for a few bars. "Don't you think that inching the top of your Barbie's bathing suit down whenever my Ken walks by so she can have 'woo-woos' for him shows that you're totally destined for 'a life of the flesh'?"

"Listen, Ag," I say. "Don't be so critical, people can play something. It doesn't mean anything."

"Yeah," she shakes her head, "sure. Let's see how long this vocation of yours lasts."

11. A Woman Might Still Have a Great Time Without Being a Nun

My Aunt Anna was nicknamed "Santa Anna" years ago cuz of the little gifts she always brings everybody any time of the year. When she comes to visit, it's like Christmas, except better. As she puts it, "There's every bit of the fun and none of the fuss." Santa Anna is so strong, and she really stands up to Uncle Mike, who's a total creep. She keeps the books in the "fine jewelry" store they run; she's really good with numbers and Michael's really not good with alcohol.

Aunt Anna is, of course, Italian, and her husband, Michael Sullivan, is an Irishman like my father. But my father says that being Irish is all he has in common with that SOB. Maybe if a man is a real SOB, God disqualifies him from being able to give love-triangle punishments to his wife, cuz Uncle Michael certainly couldn't do anything to make Aunt Anna "submissive." She gets you thinking, despite God's bizarre treatment of married women, that some of them might still discover ways to have a great time without being a nun. Possibly owning a jewelry store and looking glamorous could also be a good career option for a girl today.

Santa Anna carries a huge, straw bag, covered with woven yellow, orange, and purple straw flowers, that looks just like something Barbie would have in one of her "fun at the beach" outfit sets. That bag holds infinite amounts of irresistible things. Her beautiful Chinese collapsible fan. Tons of makeup. The presents she always brings us—especially wonderfully large costume jewelry she buys from a discount store across the street from hers. She actually prefers colored glass and paste to "fine" jewelry cuz it's big and colorful. Just like she is. Though she's large-boned, she's really tall, so her figure's excellent.

Her bag also holds all kinds of delicious foods that we always devour for lunch. A big loaf of unsliced Italian bread, cheeses, especially Asiago—which definitely doesn't stink like my father's feet—cookies, and a whole, long, skinny salami. Today the salami smells so good that my mouth starts watering before Aunt Anna even gets it out of her bag. Her salami is totally different from the stuff my mother and I get at the A&P. And we never buy anything unsliced.

Anna sees me eyeing the salami and cuts me a thick piece. The rules for eating that are strictly enforced at our house seem to change—or just disappear—when we're at Nana's. If I could eat at Nana and Pa's every night, I bet I'd never have any stomach problems. How will my stomach react to the food they eat at the nuns' house? Will I ever have salami or pignoli amoretti cookies again? Could I sneak some on the q.t.? Probably not. Cuz, as a nun, you must curb the pleasures of your senses to focus on religious things. So the food might be like what we get in the cafeteria—with all the vegetables and cooked fruit tasting like burnt sheets. Unchewable and stringy. I almost gag thinking about stuffing all that unswallowable food into my nun's napkin to throw away.

As we're about to eat, there's a knock at the door, and we hear the wonderfully deep and phlegmy voice of Aunt Maria. She's my mother's other sister—there's my mother, Elda, Santa Anna, and Aunt Maria. "Anybody home?" she calls, coughing from the cold weather and all her cigarettes. I rush to the living room to hug her. She's so skinny that I can feel her bones right through her light coat.

"I can't stay long but I knew from Nana you'd all be here, and I just had to see you this time." Then everyone is crowded around Maria. She can't get away that often from the projects where she lives in Roxbury, so her visit, which I'm sure is on the q.t. from Uncle Lou, is a real treat.

"Just in time for lunch," says Nana. Maria sits down at the table without washing her hands. "I need a cigarette first," she says, lighting one while Santa Anna cuts more of everything, and I'm so happy that I can't stop eating chunks of salami and bread and cheese.

"I'll have some of that soda Bridget's drinking and then a coffee," Aunt Maria says, and my mother jumps up to get the soda, and Santa Anna fills the espresso pot. Nana asks Anna to get three plump artichokes out of the oven where she's been secretly keeping them warm. Anna squeezes Maria from behind so suddenly that it makes her jump. She startles easily, I guess cuz Uncle Lou probably sneaks up to hit her. Anna's glancing at Maria's face on the q.t. for bruises. But I can't see any. Maybe Uncle Lou hasn't been on any benders lately.

Nana holds Maria's hand and then grabs my mother's. And Aunt Maria reaches for Santa Anna's. They gaze at each other and just laugh. They're turning into my mother's stories about them as girls. How they'd put on shows and dances for Nana and Pa's friends after the big dinner Nana cooked every Saturday night. Their girl voices could sing in harmony and they all took ballet lessons so they'd choreograph all their own moves. My mother loved those shows, even though she'd never perform in any of her own dance recitals, would throw up with her nerves. But she wasn't nervous dancing in her own house with her two sisters.

Imagine knowing each other for that long? Years and years of love. Regardless of husbands. Back before my mother had gray hair. Or Santa Anna needed creams to keep the wrinkles away. And before Aunt Maria's front teeth stuck out cuz she can't afford to go to a dentist to cure her gum disease. I think right now they're all picturing each other from years ago. You can tell by their smiles and the warmth in their watery brown eyes. My aunts always make me wish I had a sister. She'd probably be a lot more helpful than Agnes is about whether I should become a nun.

Aunt Maria's cigarette cough and the sizzle of the espresso pot spilling over bring them back to me. "So, how's my favorite niece?" Maria asks, which is a joke cuz, not counting the Staten Island relations, I'm her only niece.

Nana and my mother try to get Maria to eat more, but she can't be tempted, even by the artichoke hearts, and says I can have her helping.

"She's always been a picky eater. Even worse than you," Nana points the dull knife she's cleaning the hearts with at me.

They start teasing my mother that she must be a bad cook since I love to eat everything at Nana's. My mother's getting upset, so I say that it's all my father's fault cuz he won't let us have enough garlic. And then Anna tells Maria, who's smoking another cigarette, all about the "garlic incident" with my father.

Aunt Maria is the middle sister, but she looks the oldest cuz she gets beaten up a lot and is so poor that she can't even try to be stylish. Though, after lunch, I notice that she's wearing a fairly nice-looking dress in a shiny, lightweight, brown paisley print and nylons with not too many nicks and flat shoes. The dress is only a little short, cuz she's pretty tall, and just a tiny bit loose on her, cuz she's so scrawny. She needs a thick leather belt. But it's still pretty. Both Anna and my mother comment that Maria isn't dressed warmly enough for this time of year and offer her one of their sweaters but she shakes her head. "I didn't come here to have a fuss made over me."

I run my fingers over Aunt Anna's straw bag, which is so light and pretty in comparison to the nuns' black leather briefcases, which look like they'd be heavy even when they're empty. Anna buys a new straw bag every spring and just throws the old one away. Sister Saint Francis Xavier told me that nuns usually keep their briefcases for life. Aunt Maria's bag looks old. It's black with a little silver clasp and a short strap and is peeling in places cuz it isn't real leather. At least nuns get leather.

As we go into the living room, leaving the dishes for later, something we can never do at home, I take a closer look at Aunt Anna's outfit—a gorgeous, form-fitting, green and blue asymmetrical block-print shift with a chunky blue-green necklace, three thick bangles, an enormous ring, and long earrings—all coordinated with, but not exactly matching, her necklace. Anna hates when things are "matchy matchy" and says people only "match rather than coordinate" when they lack imagination and the courage to take a bit of a risk, whether it's on bracelets or furniture or life. Her stylish haircut is so short on the sides and back and so bushy on the top. No one we know has a relative with hair or clothes like Santa Anna's. And even though she's 5'10", she still wears big high heels. Except for when Grandpa Flaherty died and Santa Anna came to the wake in a black dress that everyone thought was too low-cut, I've never seen her wear outfits that weren't bright and alive. She also smells wonderful. Her perfumes are musky and not in the least like "Bluegrass"—the one perfume the nuns are allowed to wear—which only smells like clean.

My mother opens a box Anna has just found for her in the straw bag. It's a three-strand set of fake pearls with swirls of a green and gold glimmery substance marbleized into them. "Oh no, Anna. It's too much," my mother protests, as she often does about Santa Anna's presents.

"I think it's beautiful, mom." I run my fingers over the beads. "And if you don't like it, you can save it for me when I'm older. I love it!" I exclaim, beaming at Santa Anna. And then I remember.

"Anything in your bag of tricks for me?" asks Aunt Maria. You can tell she's not expecting a present, since her visit was a surprise.

But Santa Anna pulls out a paper bag which she tosses to Maria and blows her a kiss. It's a lovely maroon woolen scarf. Aunt Maria looks at me and chuckles, which gets her crackly cough going again. We're both wondering if that scarf was meant for me. But I don't care. My mother knits me all the scarves I need. And Maria could use anything to keep her warm in this weather.

"Catch this!" calls Anna and she tosses a lipstick to Maria. "It's just a little used because I had to try it on to be sure it matched the scarf perfectly."

Maria laughs. "You're so full of it, Anna!"

And Anna looks like she's going to cry. "I'm going to make more coffee," she says as she rushes to the kitchen.

I follow her. "Don't mind me with my pee-pee eyes," Santa Anna says. "It doesn't mean anything. It's a condition I have." And she runs to the bathroom to fix her glimmer eye shadow and sends me back into the living room, where Maria has just noticed the time and is getting ready to leave.

Maria gives me a huge hug, ties her new scarf around her neck, and heads out the door before she even finishes buttoning her coat. I don't think she's wearing any gloves.

Santa Anna brings in coffee for my mother and Nana and another glass of soda for me. She winks at me. She knows I admire her, even though today she's really making me worry about how I'll give up the prospect of wearing jewelry—real or fake. And eye shadow, which I haven't really used yet—except as pretend—for the rest of my life when I become a nun. Not to mention tight dresses and dramatic haircuts, know what I mean?

While she and my mother start arguing again about whether the shimmery pearls are too fancy, I think about that ring Santa Anna gave me that I love. It's made of white plastic with an opening in the back so it can expand as my finger grows. It holds a large stone the color of the red wine Agnes's parents drink every night on their porch at five o'clock. The stone pops out when you give the ring a squeeze and we pretend it has magical properties.

We place it in some short grass in Agnes's backyard and enter a Greek myth that we all know from the stories of my Staten Island aunts. We're Ariadne stranded by Dionysus on the island of Lemnos. And we're the virgin Amethyst who's angered Dionysus cuz she refused to return his drunken love. We plead to the goddess Diana to help us escape from the island but are condemned to wander forever in misery and be pursued by Dionysius's tigers until we find the amethyst stone that exactly fits our ring. We run and swoon all around in a state of misery, hearing the tigers roar, fearing the wrath of the drunken Dionysus, calling again and again for Diana to rescue us.

Sometimes Agnes wears a red nightie of her mother's that looks a little like Waterhouse's picture of Ariadne that's in the Greek myths book. Lucy often cries and collapses, knowing that, as Amethyst, she'll be turned into quartz by Diana, usually played by me, since the ring is mine. I can only save her from the drunken god by this radical transformation.

What a bunch of SOBs these male gods are! It doesn't matter if they're pagan or Christian—they're all jealous, demanding, and obsessed by virginity. So every one of them feels justified to treat women terribly. How have I never noticed this before?

We stay close to the stone so we don't actually lose it. Finally one of us glimpses it. Gleaming in the sun. Left for us by Diana. Cuz the stone fits perfectly into the ring, like Cinderella's foot in the glass slipper, it releases us from Dionysus, tames the tigers, turns Amethyst back into a young girl, and lets us all marry princes or stay virgins, whatever we choose. I will, I know, have to give up such games and vanities when I enter the convent.

As I watch Aunt Anna and my mother and Nana, so relaxed with each other in the cold November sun in the living room, I wonder how Anna has escaped God's wrath against married women. The Virgin Mary must be protecting her on the q.t. and doing a way better job than Diana did with Amethyst.

"So," I say as casually as I can to Aunt Anna, "do you think the Virgin Mary intercedes with God on your behalf because you guys have a special relationship or something?"

Santa Anna laughs out loud. "I don't think the Blessed Mother has anything against me, thank you very much." And with a little effort, she pulls down the neck of her dress to show me a blue Virgin Mary medal pinned to her rather large bra strap. "See? I believe in her. But Bridget, it would be wrong for me to want to be special to Mary. I'm just an ordinary woman doing fairly ordinary things." Her voice sounds a little sad. "Though I'm a pretty successful jeweler. And a good daughter and sister." She pinches my cheek. "Right?"

"Yes," I say, "and you're an incredible aunt."

She takes my hands in hers. "I pray to Mary from time to time. But what you're talking about is like wanting, I don't know, to be chums with an angel. They're in their world and we're in ours. All in all, I think it's better for me to wear my medal and then just get on with my life." She stops to glare at my mother. "Elda, why do you still have Bridget in that crazy Catholic school?" And then she mumbles something I can't hear, but I know it's disapproving of the nuns or St. Michael's, which means that one day, when I'm a nun, Santa Anna will disapprove of me. I get up, intending to leave the room, trying not to develop Aunt Anna's pee-pee eyes myself before I get to the bathroom. There's no way I'm telling her about my vocation.

But Santa Anna calls me back with one of her big smiles. "Probably the thing I do that Mary likes best, which honors her as the mother of God and that also helps me a bit," she laughs, "is to keep the jewelry store open late on Christmas Eve—til about nine p.m. That gives all the men who need last-minute 'fine' gifts for their wives one extra chance to get them. And make their wives happy." She raises her eyebrows to see if I like her answer so far and I try to smile. "So Christmas in my neck of the woods perhaps has a little more good will toward women than it otherwise would. All the while celebrating Mary's giving birth to Jesus." Santa Anna stops and looks at me again. "What d'ya think?"

I really can't imagine Mary cares if women have jewelry, know what I mean? But perhaps, just maybe, I suppose she might want wives to be happy on Christmas. "You always have everything figured out so well, Santa Anna." I reach over and give her a big kiss. She's really is a pretty impressive aunt. She not only escapes God's love-triangle punishments herself, she manages to find ways to help husbands lessen them for their wives.

"Yeah," she says. "And if Michael bothers to get in at a decent hour, we can even go to Mass this year before we come over here for Christmas." Maybe Uncle Michael keeps the jewelry store open even later than Santa Anna does.

I'm definitely looking forward to spending Christmas at Nana and Pa's with my parents and Santa Anna and her family. We don't often celebrate Christmas all together. And it is sort of Anna's name day, after all. Even though I don't like Uncle Michael or my cousin Mikey, I'll try to keep my feelings on the q.t. Above all, I'll have to practice not enjoying too many things of the world to prepare me for becoming a nun.

As much as I love the green velvet dress my mother made me, I'll stop myself from running my hands up and down it to enjoy its deep softness. I won't have any artichoke hearts, which are my favorite food in the universe, especially the way Nana cooks artichokes, with all that olive oil and fresh garlic. I can still taste them from lunch earlier. And whenever I open a present, I'll think of who I can give it away to, unless it's something like knee socks that I really need. I can probably get one of the nuns to ship most of my presents to a Catholic mission in Africa or China to give the pagan babies warm clothes and toys.

I'll also try not to enjoy any secular Christmas music that Nana will have on the record player. Every hour I'll remind myself to focus on the birth of Christ. And my vocation. On mankind's redemption. And my own.

12. Christmas Dinner: Santa Anna and the Sewer Creature

Nana and Pa's house is infused with heavenly aromas from Nana's cooking and sweet-smelling Christmas tree pine. It can't be sinful for me to breathe it in deeply. Evens nuns must notice Christmas smells. The tree blinks with colored lights, and young Italian boys sing carols on the record player. Santa Anna laughs with Nana in the kitchen while shepherds "quake at the sight" in Italian. Christmas has started.

If only Uncle Michael and my cousin Mikey didn't have to be here. Michael hasn't even said "Merry Christmas" to us. You'd think Mikey was the Christ child the way my uncle is going on.

"I'm my happiest," he says, talking to no one in particular, "with a polo shirt on, a martini in my hand, watching my little Mikey play tennis at the club." His excitement shows that he's already well into the Prosecco. My father doesn't buy special shirts to relax in. He just wears old clothes.

Even though Uncle Michael doesn't stop—he's giving stats on Mikey's winning record at the club and at college—we wish them a Merry Christmas. They don't notice us. Pa's half asleep in his chair. His cigarette ash is so long, I doubt he's touched it since he lit it. I put it out in the ashtray. Have Michael and Mike even been talking to him or just blathering on? Pa looks so fragile, like his bones could fall apart if I squeezed him. I give him a gentle kiss on his forehead. His blanket's on the floor. I lift it back over his lap and thin legs. My mother sighs then grabs our coats and hats and rushes off to put them in the spare room and I quickly follow her. There's no Christmas spirit in this room. I glance back at my father who's been cornered by Uncle Michael.

Nana and Santa Anna are busy in the kitchen, but they stop to hug us with hands sticking out so food won't get on our clothes. Aunt Anna is already wearing her Santa hat. People say Christmas is the season for children, but this is so her day, and later on she'll hand out a larger than usual collection of joke presents, one of the highlights of being with her at Christmas. Watching Santa Anna stuff chopped garlic cloves into baby artichokes, seeing Nana flute the edges of a mince pie with a motion I still can't learn, and feeling the winter sun shining in the kitchen erase Michael and Mike and make me realize how happy I am we're all spending Christmas together. I try to take everything in, realizing there won't be that many more Christmases like this, since I'll probably be in a convent by the time I'm eighteen. That only leaves six years. Half the amount of time I've already lived.

Suddenly my father appears. "I don't know how much I can stand." He thinks he's whispering to my mother but he's loud enough for everyone in the kitchen to hear. "Michael's already drunk! And Mikey seems well on his way!" He rolls his eyes.

"How can I help you?" my mother asks Nana and Santa Anna loudly, like she's trying to drown my father out.

"I think you'd better make some coffee for the two of them," my father groans, sitting heavily at the kitchen table and putting his elbow in the flour. My mother gets a clean dish towel to wipe him off, but Nana stops her and does it herself.

"Everything's under control," smiles Nana, pouring me a glass of Italian orange soda. My father shakes his head as if to say nothing's under control, but he stays silent.

"Well, can I clean anything up?" My mother's desperate to stay in the kitchen.

"No you can't," smiles Santa Anna. She's wearing dangly red and green rhinestone earrings in the shape of Christmas trees. They catch the sun so she looks trimmed with blinking lights herself. Then her eyes twinkle, and she pokes my father, tipping him off that she's about to make a joke. "No cleaning for you today on Christmas, Elda! Face it, Patrick and I know that you'd wash the soap if you had the chance."

Anna's always teasing my mother about how much she cleans. But now we all laugh at her joke, even if it is predictable. And we relax. My father even smiles and gives Anna a weak hug. I wonder how many more times I'll get to see Santa Anna make my dad laugh.

Nana says to tell Pa it's time for his lie down.

"What, on Christmas?" I complain.

"Don't fret, he'll be up for dinner." Then she says I need to visit with the Mikes, "because this kitchen is getting too crowded." I moan. This isn't exactly the Christmas I had planned.

My father looks at me sympathetically. "I'll get one of these Christmas ladies to make them some coffee and bring it in. And I'm sure I'll be thrown out of the kitchen soon too." He really is making an effort.

My father actually comes to the living room to help Pa to bed. "Hiya," I call out to the Mikes. At first they don't say anything to me. They're too engrossed in the card game they're playing on the sofa—they didn't even bother getting the card table out—to notice me. "Watcha playin'?" I ask, trying to sound enthusiastic.

"Cards," says Mikey and they both laugh. Like I'm some kind of idiot. Uncle Mike coughs as he takes a drag of his cigarette, and I notice he's using one of Nana's good saucers as an ashtray.

"Listen, honey," he croaks, finally looking up at me, "this is a game for older people. Plus only two can play." They look at each other and snicker. Some kind of mutual admiration society card game, I'm sure. As if I'd want to play with them anyway.

So I just sit in the living room and try not to scowl. They are two people I won't miss when I'm a nun. And I won't pray for them either. Well, I suppose I'll have to. Finally Uncle Michael asks if I can get them "a fresh bottle of bubbly." I delight in saying, "No, Nana's making you both some coffee, and my dad'll bring it in when it's ready."

"Who the hell wants coffee?" Uncle Michael's words are faintly slurred. "That Italian stuff your grandmother makes would burn a hole right through a man's stomach. It's not even like real coffee. It's only fit for Italians to drink. And more than that, I really don't think Mikey here is old enough to be drinking strong coffee."

I want to say that what Nana makes is authentic espresso. Even my father admits that. Plus if Uncle Michael thinks Mikey's old enough to drink Prosecco, which is also Italian, not letting him have coffee doesn't even make sense.

But then they both start chuckling again, their shoulders going up and down, and their faces turn Irish red. It finally dawns on me that Uncle Michael's made a joke at my expense that they think is hysterical. How can Santa Anna stand them? I decide not to reply, but I do bring over Pa's ashtray and clear my throat as I take the saucer away from them. It's evil how disrespectful they are to Nana.

"What are you fiddling about with, girl?" says Mikey. "Leave us alone." I do leave. To wash the saucer out in the bathroom. I don't want Nana or Santa Anna to see what Uncle Michael has done. The smell of stale smoke gets up my nose once the water hits the dish, and it makes me feel kind of nauseous. The ashes stick under my fingernails as I scrape the plate clean. I hate them both.

My cousin Mikey is a history major in college, and I swear he learns historical facts just so he can come home and make us all look stupid by telling us things we don't know. He's probably brought some history lessons as Christmas presents that he'll treat us to at dinner. You can see just by the way he holds his head that he thinks he's better than his family, not only cuz he's in college and has learned more history than the rest of us have, but he has a tennis scholarship and is supposedly the most brilliant tennis player at his school. Though we don't really have proof that he is. And I think his grades are pretty crap, but Uncle Michael keeps that on the q.t.

Mikey's played tennis for as long as I can remember, and he's always said he's going to be a star. "When I grow up my picture'll be on the front pages of the sports sections of every newspaper," he used to brag to me as he was slamming a tennis ball back and forth against their garage door, "and you'll just become some dumb housewife."

I'm not old enough yet to look smarter than Mikey, but I'm sure I am, even if I can't play tennis. And the whole idea of his picture in the paper reminds me of Sylvia DeStephano, her modeling career, and her possession by the Devil. Mikey has seemed possessed for years. Nobody, except someone with evil powers, could hit a ball back and forth that many times without missing.

Finally Pa gets up from his nap. He looks smaller than before. But at least we're sitting down to dinner. As I eat a few artichoke leaves with lovely garlic and olive oil (I still plan to abstain from any of the hearts) and have some spaghetti, I can see that dinner will be so delicious, and I realize how hungry I am. And then there'll be the presents. Unfortunately there are also three bottles of red wine set out for dinner, and when Pa does the toast, most everyone takes a nice sip, but the Mikes drain their glasses and pour themselves refills immediately. They're drinking their second glasses quickly too, even though Pa tells them to take it easy.

Right in the middle of Nana's explaining how she makes eggplant parmigiana, Uncle Michael starts on about Aunt Anna's nickname. He's so rude cuz Nana was talking about the importance of soaking the eggplant in salt water to get rid of its bitterness, which is really interesting. Plus she's been cooking for days and deserves respect, even if you find the subject of eggplants boring.

"She isn't called Santa Anna because she's like Santa Claus, lemme tell you," says Uncle Michael, raising his third-in-a-series-of-already-way-too-many-glasses-of-wine to toast Aunt Anna. "She's Santa Anna because she's like the Santa Ana winds—fast, hot, and dangerous." Uncle Michael sounds like he's joking, but his gray-blue eyes are angry as well as kind of bloodshot.

Anna adjusts herself in her chair. "That's enough, Michael." She smiles at us and frowns at him, but her voice is unflustered. "What's the matter with you? People can't be warm and loving without being 'hot' and 'dangerous'? What a silly thing to say, especially on Christmas." She purses her Christmas-red lips at Michael and opens a button on her blouse so you can really see her woo-woos and leans over for a kiss. But Uncle Michael brushes her away. Her nose and eyes are instantly as red as her lips. Why doesn't she put that disgusting drunk in his place?

"No, it isn't enough, Anna, not nearly," he slurs, leaning on the back legs of his chair. "Let's toast Santa Ana, a forest fire—burning and burning 'til nothing's left."

What's he talking about? My Santa Anna is not a woman who puts up with insults like this from her husband. She doesn't submit to Michael. She should knock him over. He's teetering in that chair. I know I would. It wouldn't take much.

Finally she pounds on his shoulder with her fists. But way too lightly. "You're the one whose 'burnt up' and 'burnt out,' but it's none of my doing." Good for her. I lay my fork down to watch what she'll do next.

"Eat your dinner before it gets cold," my mother, who's sitting next to me, says softly. But how can I eat? Santa Anna's eyes are beginning to tear up. She can't cry. Not on Christmas. She always says you shouldn't cry in front of men, both cuz it'll ruin your makeup and cuz it makes them think you're weak, which if you are, you better keep that information on the q.t. And Santa Anna is anything but weak.

"Oh, I'm burnt up, baby. A has-been. Everyone knows that. A big disappointment to your family here." Uncle Michael nods vaguely to everyone around the table. Well, I'm glad he's aware of what we all think of him. Just one little shove and he'd lose his balance and be sprawled across the floor. "But even they'd have to agree that the cause behind the little man was the big woman. I mean, what man isn't allowed to open the till of his own store register?" He drinks another glass of wine down in one big gulp.

"A drunk and a thief, that's who!" I'm planning to yell out. But as if my mother senses this, she puts her arm around me and moves her finger to her lips. "This is between them. Not a word out of you."

What kind of attitude is that? You don't defend your own sister on Christmas? It's a wife-punished-by-God-into-submission attitude. At least when I'm a nun that'll never happen to me. I'll get a special leave to come home just to tell him what I really think of him, the SOB. Aunt Anna and I don't think women should accept abuse from men just cuz they're your husband. We're strong and won't let men push us around. I can't believe that my mother is so "subject to her husband" that she isn't going to say something to put that creep in his place.

I look down at what was, until moments ago, a delicious Christmas dinner—lamb chops from a crown roast, asparagus frittata, candied yams—and try to think of something I can say to at least change the subject when suddenly there's more shouting. Anna is trying to kiss Uncle Michael again, but this time he gives her a real shove and almost knocks her off her chair.

"Get away from me, you old hag. You think I'm fooled by mutton dressed as lamb? That opening your shirt is attractive? At your age? You're revolting, Anna. You disgust me." And he starts looking around for the bottle to fill his empty wine glass.

Even though it's pretty obvious that Uncle Michael has had way too much to drink, everyone seems in shock that he'd say something so horrible out loud to Santa Anna. And in front of all of us. And on Christmas. Nana is staring straight ahead, expressionless. Pa is extremely pale and looks like he might pass out. My mother's fiddling with her napkin. Even my father's flushed, and his lips are narrowed, the way they get when he's really mad.

The room is silent for a minute until finally Anna dimly says, "What?" She looks so stunned.

"What do you mean, 'What'?" Michael chides. "Like you don't know. I'm stuck in this damn web with you because we're Catholics. Not that I believe in any of it. But the Church always wins."

Santa Anna's red lips are trembling but she still manages not to cry. She keeps her eyes on Uncle Michael and talks softly to him. "But we made Mikey together. Your little Mikey that you love more than anything in the world. He was worth it all, right, Mike?" Her voice is getting more and more tender when what he needs is a solid left hook to the jaw. I'd certainly be willing to take a swing.

"Mike?" Santa Anna calls out to him again with eager-looking eyes. Disgusting, if you ask me. How can she be begging him? My powerful Aunt Anna. And using my cousin Mikey as an example of something good? He's more of a reason against getting married. Stuck-up little shit.

"Yeah, yeah. Mikey's worth everything. Especially when I can get him away from you."

Then Mikey, who's sitting on Santa Anna's other side, turns to her and smiles. That's unusual. And he puts his hand on her shoulder. And she leans her head over and grabs his hand, kisses it, and keeps holding on to it. This is so degrading. I don't trust him. Why does she?

"Ma," his voice sounds all soft and pleasant, "you gotta admit, you were great for stuff like making sure I was always at tennis practice on time when I was a kid. Dad and I'll both give you that." She nods like she feels some sense of pride in him, and she looks a little brighter. "Don't trust him!" I want to scream at her.

Then Mikey sits up straighter and laughs. "Look at you now, though, Ma. You're such an embarrassment with your tight clothes and shiny tan. It's like you still imagine that you're twenty or something. Why d'you think I never bring any friends home? Who'd want them to see you?" Santa Anna doesn't move a muscle. How can she take so much viciousness and cruelty?

Then I remember that in the Bible even Jesus is disrespectful to his mother. The Blessed Virgin Mary. The Queen of Queens. When they ran out of wine at that Marriage of Cana, Mary suggested that he make some miracle wine, since he was the Son of God and everything. And it was like the first time she ever asked him for anything. But what'd he do? Act like he didn't give two hoots for her. "Woman, what is it to me? My hour is not yet come." Oh, excuse me, Jesus. I suppose Mary didn't have her special watch on that day, the one that would chime when your "hour" had come. Bet she didn't think it was her hour when Gabriel showed up either, but she was respectful and obedient, know what I mean?

Jesus did give in eventually and changed the water into wine. Still for a while he seemed like he didn't care about his mother at all. I'm sure that after he said those cruel words, Mary must have looked just the way Santa Anna does right now. I'm so glad I'm not going to have children. That no one'll ever be able to hurt me like this. Mikey is such a strong reason for becoming a nun.

While I'm thinking about what an SOB Jesus was to Mary, Santa Anna rushes from the Christmas dinner table, and Nana follows her into the bathroom. The rest of us sit there. Silently. Anna is sobbing something about how Michael's stealing more jewelry from her store and says next year she'll fill it all with fakes so he can't rob her anymore.

I feel dizzy. The room is spinning. I crumble into my chair. How stupid I was to imagine that any wife, even my Santa Anna, could escape the wrath of her husband, the wrath of God. He said: "Let the women learn in silence with all subjection." There's no way He'll let a woman win over her husband. If Santa Anna takes away the keys to the cash register, God will just allow Uncle Michael to take a lot more away from her. Like her dignity. "I suffer not a woman to teach, nor to usurp authority over the man, but to be in silence." Silence. I want to scream. I'm glad Santa Anna isn't silent, but obviously God's not pleased. Even if you're fighting such a loser like Uncle Michael. I'd become a nun right now, if this Christmas dinner would just end.

"Everyone still has it wrong," says Mikey as if we were having a normal meal. The smirk on his face means we're in for our Christmas history lesson. And here I was thinking things couldn't get any worse. "My mother's named after Antonio Lopez de Santa Anna, the leading villain of Texas." Mikey laughs at his own joke. No one else knows what he's talking about. And who cares about Texas anyway? "Santa Anna was elected president of Mexico and then became a dictator. That's my mother, popular on the outside, but a dictator on the inside." Mikey and Uncle Michael lock eyes and laugh. I wish that something would happen. A small kitchen fire. A power outage. Anything.

"There's this one fact about Santa Anna that's Mother to a T," Mikey sniggers and sort of drools. You can tell he's had way too much to drink. Like father, like son. "He was a lousy fighter, and in one battle in 1842 he lost his leg, which was then buried. He became friends with people in high places and got them to have a huge ceremony to..." and he stops to check that we're all paying attention. In the quiet I can hear Aunt Anna crying with Nana in the bathroom. Mikey must hear her too.

"Okay, so get this." He looks at each of us. "Santa Anna convinced people to dig up the remains of his leg. Then he made them have a parade, carrying his rotten leg all through Mexico City. In the end it was actually put on public display." He pauses, waiting for everyone to laugh at his disgusting story. Nobody says anything, so he laughs.

"Don't you love the sheer self-centeredness of it?" exclaims Mikey, his alcoholic voice rising. "After all," he continues, his words slurring like his father's, "how many thousands of men lose limbs in battle? But this Santa Anna guy had an ego so big." and Mikey opens his arms wide, nearly hitting my mother in the face, "that he convinced people to find his stupid leg, dig it up, and worship it, like it was some kind of relic or something."

Mikey looks around the table, his eyes dilated. "Isn't that like our Santa Anna, always needing to be the center of attention? Always showing off? Always trying to con people into loving her? We just about have to stop living if she loses an earring. Can you imagine if she lost a leg?" Mikey just won't stop.

Uncle Michael's whole body is shaking up and down with laughter. He gets up and pats Mikey on the back. "You're rich, kid. You sure can tell it like it is." He grabs a wine bottle from the sideboard to pour Mikey another glass when Pa, who never raises his voice, cries out, "Enough! I want a Christmas in peace." That shuts Mikey up, but the dinner and the whole day are ruined.

Aunt Anna does eventually come out of the bathroom and play her role, handing out all the Christmas presents with her Santa hat on. She doesn't even forget the packets of fake twenties she usually puts in everyone's cards or stockings, even though they annoy my father so much. "It's just a sign of how they squander their real money," he says on the q.t. to my mother, as if it was her fault.

But after we all open our gifts, Aunt Anna starts to cry again and runs out of the room. This time my mother as well as Nana go with her, and I see them head for the back bedroom. Uncle Michael's dozing in the easy chair in the living room. Mikey's on the phone with his girlfriend, and my father's watching the news on TV, waiting to leave. So it's easy enough for me to slip away and stand outside the half-open bedroom door and listen. As they talk, I quietly push the door a little more so I have a clearer view of Anna on the bed and Nana and my mother sitting beside her.

"I'd had enough of his missing the toilet when he's drunk and puking all over the floor. Especially since last week, when he was so confused he peed in the closet," Santa Anna begins. "I bought some fake vomit from the joke shop as a Christmas Eve present, but it didn't look realistic enough. So I put bits of a hamburger and small pieces of boiled potatoes and carrots on it. Then I added a little ketchup—just a bit here and there to help the consistency."

"It must have been pretty funny when he came home and found it. Smart of you to make your point with a little humor," Nana says, trying, I guess, to sound encouraging.

"The bastard, of course, was too sloshed last night to even notice it," Anna sobs. "Imagine coming home that drunk on Christmas Eve? And the diamond pendant from the store? Gone, of course. He gave it to her for Christmas." My mother and Nana look at each other, but neither seems able to say anything to that.

I used to think Aunt Anna was calling Uncle Michael a "basket," and that seemed funny. Now I know what she's really saying.

"So I left the vomit there until this morning. He wakes me up at five screaming bloody murder, calling me to come quick, that some kind of sewer creature, like a jellyfish, had crawled out of the toilet, and he'd just stepped on it."

Nana bursts into laughter. I'm sure she's picturing Uncle Michael with the fake throw-up and ketchup and squashed potatoes stuck to his foot. "Serves him right."

"I'm leaving him, Mom," Anna weeps. "I've had enough of Michael and his women." Then she sits up straight and glares at Nana. "I might as well say it. What's the point of 'making nice' all the time, like you tell us?" My mother puts her arms around Anna, trying to calm her down. "I will say it!" Anna cries out defiantly, shaking her off. "His women get the real jewelry and the real money. I'm just stuck— the clown—with everything fake." Then she grabs Nana by the shoulders and screams, "And Ma, face it. It's my marriage that's the biggest fake."

Nana seems not to be listening but keeps laughing at Michael. "A sewer creature. What an idiot."

But my mother isn't laughing. She looks at Nana sternly. "Wait, Ma, you always said we have to go back to our husbands, no matter what they do. Did you hear Anna? She says she's leaving Michael. Remember all the times I came over when I first married Patrick? You wouldn't let me in the front door, even though his father was such a bastard and I was in tears. You remember, right?"

I've heard the horrible story of my mother's honeymoon many times, but I didn't know she actually tried to leave my father before I was around. Not that I can really blame her. Her wedding night must have been her first love-triangle punishment—a special wedding present from God-the-F. She and my father spent their honeymoon night in his bedroom in Grandpa and Uncle Joe's apartment because they couldn't afford to go away.

Nana had made my mother a silk satin floor-length nightgown trimmed with delicate lace and appliques in a lovely cream color with a matching chiffon and lace robe. Once in a while, my mother takes it out of her hope chest, and we look at it together and touch it. It's probably the most gorgeous outfit I've ever seen. Nana spent months creating it, and all by hand, but my mother wore it only that one night.

In the morning, after my mother had stayed with my father in his room—and she told me she didn't get much sleep because he snored so loudly—she tiptoed into the kitchen resplendent in her beautiful nightgown and robe to make everyone some coffee, and before she even saw him, my grandfather screamed at her: "You creature of sin! You temptress! You defilement! Get away from my sight and never come out that door without being fully clothed. And when you're dressed this morning, go to the priest and confess your sins."

My mother became hysterical, and they had to get Nana to come over and calm her down. But Nana told her that once you were married, that was it. So my poor, lovely mother had to learn about God's enmity to married women the very first morning she woke up joined in wedlock to my father, even though he was still too in love with her to dish out any himself. 'Course, that's definitely changed. I'll never let any of this happen to me.

She's still yelling at Nana. "And you forbid Maria to leave that son of a bitch, even when she comes over with a black eye."

My mother never goes to Nana's after she and my father have a big fight now. She runs out, slams the upstairs door and then the downstairs front door, screaming that she's "never coming back." I realize that she most likely won't go further than the next block, cuz she and my father have to hear each other so they can continue their fight from the street.

She yells up to him, and he opens the screen in the living room and sticks his head out and shouts at her. And meanwhile I'm screaming silently to myself, sitting on the floor in a corner because she never takes me with her. Never. Not once. And I'd go in a second. She always comes back but still says that she'd be gone if she had a driving license. And I guess, she'd also need to have her own car. Maybe she would. Just drive away and I'd never see her again. And my father and I would be left alone, which makes me so unhappy whenever they have one of those fights that I can't stop throwing up for days.

But 'course I don't tell my mother I'm so sad that she doesn't take me whenever she runs away. I don't want to upset her any further. Maybe I'd let her know if she had a license and I thought she'd really go.

"Anna's not going to leave anyone," whispers Nana softly to my mother. "But we have to give her time to cry it all out and tell her stories, especially when they're so funny." Then she turns back to Anna, holding her face tightly. "I can't get over it, Anna. Michael, Mr. I'm-so-sophisticated-in-my-clothes-for-the-club, actually thinking that a 'sewer creature' had jumped out of the toilet." I can see her trying to make Anna take it all more lightly now.

She picks up a hairbrush and runs it through Anna's hair. Her voice is as gentle as her brushing. "Michael always appreciates a good joke. And he's not a stupid fellow." She smiles at Anna, putting the brush down, "I definitely think that joke shop must be slipping if that old looker of a husband of yours mistook vomit for a sewer creature." Nana glances back and forth between my mother and Anna. "I trained my three girls well. All of you. My princesses always go back to their princes."

Nana looks out the door at me, staring right into my eyes. "C'mon in, Bridey," and she gives me a hug. "I know you've been out there listening because you're worried about Santa Anna." This is a gracious way of remarking that I've been eavesdropping. Even though she keeps talking to me, what Nana says seems meant for Aunt Anna. "You don't have to worry, Bridget. These little problems always happen in a marriage."

Anna is shaking her head and starts crying again. "No, Ma, no. Not this time."

You go, Anna, I tell her in my heart, and I reach out to touch her hand. But Nana moves in front of me so I can't. She takes my hand and continues to speak slowly and easily. "Just try to remember, Bridget, it's like when you had the chicken pox when you were seven. You felt so terrible and itchy that scratching was all you could think about. But then you got better, and you probably don't even remember that chicken pox much anymore."

I feel the bridge of my nose toward my right eye—the one small scar the chicken pox left. I don't say anything.

"Or what about the mumps?" Nana asks. "I'll bet you hardly ever think about them either, right?" When I got the mumps, Santa Anna arrived with a blonde wig and sunglasses for me. "You probably feel like hell, but you might as well try looking like Marilyn Monroe. At least that's what I always do," she smiled at me in orange-lipped delight, the corners of her navy-blue-outlined-fading-into-glittery-sky-blue eyes squeezing tightly as she pulled the wig onto my head, her knuckles making me wince a little as they touched my swollen glands. She pressed her lips hard against my cheek and that also hurt, but it was worth it to get a kiss from Santa Anna.

"And," Nana shrugs, "one of these days, the measles. You'll feel terrible all over again, but then you get better and forget them too."

So does Nana think marriage is like going through a series of childhood diseases? She pinches my arm and nods at me. I'm not getting off scot-free for eavesdropping after all. She expects me, for whatever reason, to take her side against my wonderful Santa Anna.

"Yes, Nana, you're right," I start slowly cuz I think she's dead wrong. "I hardly think about the chicken pox at all now." I know that Uncle Michael is not like the chicken pox. He's a whole plague of diseases and pestilences and locusts and frogs sent by God-the-F to just one person, my poor Aunt Anna.

Nana starts squeezing my shoulder, raises her eyebrows, and smiles expectantly. What I said isn't sufficient.

My stomach clenches. Nana glares at me. "And right now," I finally mumble, "I'm not worried about getting the measles." Still tightening her hand on my shoulder, continuing her insistent look, Nana steps on my foot! Not enough yet?

"When I do catch the measles, I'm sure I'll be really sick, but everyone will take care of me and I'll get better." I feel like Judas. Nana gives me a big grin and a hug. I said everything she wanted. Even though it was all so dishonest.

"What's the expression?" Nana asks. "Out of the mouths of babes?" She nods and finally lets go of me and cuddles Santa Anna. I'm not a babe. And those words didn't just come out of my mouth. Nana made me speak them. "Anna, you need to listen to our Bridget here." Why does she think something will be good for Anna just cuz I said it? And why should Anna think so?

Finally Nana goes into the living room and announces quite loudly, "Time for everyone to go now. Back to their husbands and their children and their own homes."

When my father hears this, he rushes up with our coats in his arms and his own already on. "Right you are," he says to Nana, giving her a hurried kiss. "Well past a lot of people's bedtimes," and he hands us our coats and scarfs. "Elda will pick up the presents tomorrow," he calls as he moves us out of the bedroom and through the dining room. I glance into the living room. Pa and Uncle Michael and Mikey are all sound asleep. Anna is still in the bedroom. There isn't anyone to say good-bye to but Nana. She pats us and gives a tired smile but pushes us out the door as quickly as my father is. It doesn't seem right to say, "Merry Christmas." We're on the porch before I've even finished buttoning my coat for our five block walk home.

What an unbearable day it's been. How did all those words get said out loud? And on Christ's birthday? I think about God-the-F and my vocation as a nun.

What He says about Eve in the Bible shows He must really hate women—"Worst of all evils is that of a woman... In woman was sin's beginning, and because of her we all die." How could God say that? No matter how mad He was all those eons ago at Eve for showing Adam her woo-woos?

We just learned in school that the Virgin Mary's called "the Sorrowful Mother"—I assumed because her son was crucified. But what if it's not only that? What if she's sorrowful because she is a woman? Why did He make her sorrowful when she agreed to everything He and Gabriel wanted? Mary's supposed to be the opposite of Eve, but I bet she had childbirth pain just like everyone else. Bastard. She must have been miserable, especially with only germy animals in a cold and filthy manger to keep the three of them from freezing to death.

How can I possibly become a nun and His bride? I won't do it, I sob into my scarf. He's just as bad as Uncle Michael to create all this suffering for innocent women. The wind blows fiercely, making my eyes ache with the cold. His eyes are cold, looking down on all our miseries. But where is Anna's evil? Where's my mother's? Or Aunt Maria's? Where is anyone's mother's evil? Where is mine? Why did he create women only to hurt and reject us?

Even Christ called out on the cross, "My God, My God, why have You forsaken me?" Though, as terrible as the crucifixion was, Jesus knew that he'd be up and about in three days. But women have been abandoned by God forever. Ever since Eve. What choices do they have?

"My girls are all good girls," Nana says. Maybe she knows we have no choices. "They realize that marriage is for better or worse. And they always go back." And they did. For a long time. Staying with their husbands through thick and thin. Through enmity after enmity. Even if they were baskets. Or childhood diseases. Even if they were sewer creatures.

But that's not going to be me. Not a nun. Not a "good girl" wife. I renounce you, God-the-F because I know you've already renounced me.

13. At the Kitchen Window IV:
The Blue Gate

From the kitchen window I can see the dilapidated house a block away, separated from us only by the large yard of our neighbors across the street. When we ride bikes, Agnes, Donna, and I always pretend the house is haunted. It has all the ingredients. Bats do actually fly out of partly boarded-up windows in the attic. At the back, there's a gate with a broken hinge that swings back and forth in the wind, making a horrible squeaking sound, punctuated by bangs as it hits the fence again and again. Every so often we think we see movement behind a window, though it's probably just a reflection from something outside.

One day, when my friends are busy and I'm alone, I decide to walk over to the house by myself. Oddly, it seems less scary closer up than it does when I'm speeding by on my bike. As I open the gate to walk into the backyard, I notice faint traces of blue paint on the gate and what's left of the fence. It seems such a bright color for a fence. I try to imagine all of it, freshly painted, and wonder if maybe the previous owners grew blue morning glories to climb up the pickets. For a while I don't want to leave the gate. Far from being haunted, it's all so empty. When I touch a bit of the blue paint, it flakes off onto my finger. I should brush it away but I can't.

Because in a moment, I know what it means. Someone had once loved the place—the house, the yard, and even the fence. They had, after all, painted it this unusual blue. They probably had a beautiful garden. Roses. Lilies of the valley. Phlox. They raked the leaves. Swept the porch. Touched up the fence. Fixed the gate. Weeded the garden. Washed the windows. And now? Now no one loves it. In an instant anyone could see. Love doesn't go on forever.

I run home and put the flake of paint on a piece of cotton in a tiny box in my sock drawer. I open it regularly to remind myself.

Sometimes I sit at the kitchen window and stare across the yard at the broken-down fence. When I try really hard, I can see the fence when it was newly painted. Safe. Covered in flowers. Bright. Loved. Happy. Like me. Winning more prizes every year. Essay contests. Science fairs. Smiling from ear to ear. Bright. Loved. Happy. "The best," my father now says, "the best."

But when I sit at the kitchen window during a storm, I open my little box and stare at that sliver of blue paint. I look out and can see the gate, but not the traces of blue. And for just an instant, I am the fleck of paint. Splintered. The fence. Abandoned. The trace of blue. Invisible. Unrecognizable, even through a window that has just been washed.

The gate is pulled wide open by the wind. Then slammed back, banging into the fence. Over and over. I can't hear the banging, because our window is closed and the rain is noisy, but I can feel it. I need to eat more. Spit out less. Forget about God-the-F and stupid love triangles. And enmity. And my lost vocation. Not be so preoccupied with how bad my parents' marriage is. Calm down. Have some faith in myself. But do what I'm told. Because I need to stay loved. I can't stop watching. That gate—

aimlessly opening and closing. Rocking back and forth. At the window. In the kitchen. With no one to see the paint peeling. No one even remembering the blue. Just rocking. Then nothing.

It's a sin to want to die, to see yourself even for a moment like that. I wonder if it's also a sin to feel dead. While you're still alive. With the paint chip. And the gate. With no latch. In the storm. At the window. In that moment. Now. And at the hour of our death.

14. Practice Boyfriend

I certainly didn't intend to become interested in an older, balding, somewhat overweight, rather short man with two prominent blackheads on his left cheek who is sort of my Aunt Maria's boyfriend. Yet there's something about him that both Aunt Maria and I find inexplicably attractive.

Mr. Vieri and his mother live across the street from me. He must be at least forty or maybe even fifty. And I'm only thirteen. But I have to admit, that man takes my mind off everything that's been bothering me. My family's never associated much with the Vieris cuz my father doesn't really want us to expand our Italian acquaintances beyond my mother and her rather sprawling family. But we get to know the Vieris when my mother's sister Maria moves in with us for the summer. She needed to escape from Uncle Lou, to recover from the injuries she suffered when he threw her down three flights of stairs. When Aunt Maria first arrived, Uncle Lou showed up at our house most every night. He stood outside, crying and usually drunk, making an embarrassing spectacle of himself and our whole family. No keeping anything about their life on the q.t. anymore in our neighborhood.

"Maria, Maria," he called until she came out on the porch or at least to the window. "Maria," he sobbed, "I'm sorry." 'Course when she didn't respond, he shook his fist at her. "You know I'm sorry! Say you know." Lou's cries could quickly take on a menacing tone. My father usually pulled Maria inside and started shutting the windows, even though it was hot, just so she wouldn't have to hear him. That got Uncle Lou going all over again. "Mari-a," he sang, "I love you so with a-all my ha-a-art." If singing didn't work, he tried blasphemy: "Maria, I love you more than God himself." That usually brought her back to the window telling him not to say anything that could land him in hell—as if he wasn't going already—but he'd just be happy she was talking to him again.

And sometimes he screams. "Ma-reee-yaaa!" The birds in the trees, scarcely settled down to sleep in their nests, startle and squawk, and fly all around as if to warn us that this man can destroy the peace of any home, even theirs.

But Uncle Lou is used to talking over the cries of others. "You know, Maria," he says, "drinking is the curse of the Irish." Sometimes he gets down on one knee or begins speaking with a bit of a brogue. "And now you've left me, my bonnie lass, I'm even more cursed." His move into the brogue is usually the breaking point for my father, who then opens the window to tell Lou to get the hell home.

Once Lou's gone, Maria bursts into tears. "What if Lou really means to change this time? Let me go after him." And then, from raising her voice, her cigarette cough gets started.

My mother, and sometimes my father, has to physically restrain her. 'Course they're gentle cuz her ribs are still bruised. Maria's left Lou many times, but she always goes back to him. Though because she had to stay in the hospital for a whole week after this last fight, my parents're trying to convince her to separate from Lou permanently, my mother having changed her mind about sticking with your husband through thick and thin when she realized that Maria could get killed.

In the end, though, it isn't my parents who help Maria leave Uncle Lou, but Mr. Vieri. Cuz Maria's with us, we get to know the Vieris, and I begin to feel very excited whenever I see Mr. V. (V. to his friends, though his real name is Alfredo). Or even when I think about him, know what I mean? Agnes introduced me to the word frisson, and her rather vulgar interpretation of it as a penis. I look it up in the big library dictionary and learn that it's a kind of intense excitement, and in my interpretation, that also means possessing a ubiquitous sexual energy. That summer Maria and I learn that Mr. V. has that kind of energy. 'Course maybe I just have it whenever I see him.

The day I feel my first frisson with Mr. V. is a warm and muggy Sunday morning, the kind when you wake up early—even though Sunday could be a great day to sleep in—cuz you want to get church out of the way before it gets even hotter. My family is leaving church when Mrs. Vieri calls out to my mother, "Elda! Elda! I want to talk to you about your roses!"

"Keep walking," my father says sternly, grabbing my mother's arm and mine and moving us along quickly. "They're just being nosy about Maria. You can still see traces of her black eye."

Then Maria calls out to us. My father didn't hurry her along, and Mrs. V. catches up to her and is introducing Maria to her son.

"We have to go back now, Patrick," my mother says firmly, "or we'll look rude."

"I don't care about looking rude," my father grumbles, sounding as if he's about to become quite rude, "but I'd rather Maria not spread her stories all over the neighborhood."

I find the Vieris a perplexing and interesting mother-son pair and am happy for any excuse to see them, even if my father's told me many times that they're low class. He really just means Italian. And so, for three very different reasons, my mother, my father, and I all walk back that Sunday to join the Vieris and Aunt Maria.

Mr. V.'s blue eyes, deep and always a little sad-looking, contrast with his contented smile as he holds Aunt Maria's elbow and gazes too closely at the bruising around her eye. He's wearing an eggshell-colored suit that's just a bit tight for him everywhere, and I mean everywhere. Mrs. V. has, as usual, taken over the conversation. She's wearing one of her many broad-brimmed straw hats that drive my father to distraction. He always calls her "the talking lampshade." Her hat, suit, purse, and shoes are all bright turquoise with black trim. She prides herself on many things, but especially on having every bit of an outfit match exactly. Probably Santa Anna would, for once, side with my father cuz we all know how she hates "matchy matchy" which really is the essence of Mrs. V. Today her wrinkled cleavage is showing more than usual, and she and Maria seem to be taking a special interest in it. Mrs. V. is showing Aunt Maria her "bunny," a plump cotton ball doused in perfume that she places between her breasts on hot days so that whenever she perspires, she activates the perfume. Maria seems enchanted. 'Course my father's ready to explode, having a very q.t. attitude about cleavages—wrinkled or not. He used to even complain when my Barbie's tops were too low cut. We're lucky he's not a violent man like Uncle Lou.

At first we only see the Vieris on Sundays, and it doesn't take long for Maria and me to start noticing that Mrs. V. is quite embarrassing—when she passes young Father McCabe or any nice-looking younger man, she often says things like, "He can put his shoes under my bed any day." Mr. V. is way more reserved and much more exciting to be with. My father often talks to the priest after Mass, asking him advice about Uncle Lou or his own war-wounded brother. So, thankfully, he misses most of Mrs. V.'s comments.

He also doesn't immediately notice how Aunt Maria and I are both becoming attracted to Mr. V. Over the next few weeks, as we come out of church, Mr. Vieri calls out to my aunt—"Maaaa-rIa?" His voice sounds so different from Uncle Lou's. He puts one arm around her and one around my mother or me, though as the Sundays pass, his arm increasingly goes around me. And then he tilts his face close to Maria's and says softly, but just loudly enough for me to hear, his hand now under my arm, gently grazing the side of my small but developing breast, "Maria, how you tempt me. Those potent bedroom eyes. You know you shouldn't come to Mass so early just out of bed." "Potent" is one of Mr. V.'s special frisson words. I get the shivers just hearing him say it.

"Oh, V., stop it. I never know what you're talking about," laughs Maria, pushing him away. Despite her words, I know she can feel something. Whenever Maria steps away from V., she looks like she's aching to move back closer. And so, I realize, am I.

Soon Maria knows she has to start meeting V. in a more discreet place than the parish green, so she finds excuses to visit him—bringing his mother flowers she cuts from our garden, something we usually never do. Or needing to borrow eggs that she just can't seem to find in our refrigerator. My mother reminds Maria more than once that she's still a married woman, and soon she won't let Maria visit the Vieris alone. She tells me, with a concerned look, that I have to go with Maria as a kind of chaperone. This suits me just fine.

The Vieris have a teak swing and matching table on their porch that V. made ages ago. In the summer his mother always puts a big, ice-filled, sweating pitcher of lemonade on the table with glasses of various sizes and shapes. The three of us sit on the swing, V. in the middle, with his arms around both of us. He wears pants and a sleeveless undershirt. His Bay Rum aftershave gives off a faint aroma that I associate with sex, even though I don't know whether sex has a smell or what it actually might smell like. The only thing I know for certain is that Agnes says it definitely does, but I'm not asking her any details cuz everything about V. is obviously on the q.t.

I'm pretty sure that V. is trying to feel my breast, so I move as close to him as I can. Aunt Maria is doing the same on the other side. I can barely breathe but my aunt is carrying on a conversation as if sitting in this level of frisson is completely normal. 'Course she's teasing V., saying that this morning she walked around the whole apartment nude cuz it's so hot—which I know she didn't, because my father won't allow any indecent displays under his roof and certainly not in public view—and that she looked at her eyes in the mirror and couldn't see what was "bedroom-y" about them at all.

V. appears to respond with total seriousness. "When a person gets up in the morning, Maria, and they aren't fully awake, their eyes have a sort of droop to them." He looks over at me, squeezes my arm and grazes my nipple with his middle finger and winks. I feel myself getting warmer, and it has nothing to do with the weather.

I'm never sure how much V. is saying to Maria and how much he's saying to me. He often finds an innocent way to lean over to get something next to me, and he just slightly loses his grip on whatever it is so that he ends up touching the inside of my leg or my hand; or sometimes he holds my gaze for a fraction longer than necessary, looking deep into my eyes.

"A droop?" my aunt says with fake indignation. "Like you're deformed or something?" She lightly punches his chest and then starts pinching him a little lower. "Well V., for a man who says certain things, you can make a woman feel as if—"

"No, no, you tantalizing Miss Bedroom Eyes." V. laughs, letting go of me. He raises his hands as if to defend himself, finding ways to quickly skim his fingers against so many parts of Maria's body. I'm tingling all over.

And then we see my father coming across the street. V. stands up.

"So, cutting the grass today, Al?" my father asks casually. I can see that he's clenching his teeth.

"More like making hay," Maria says under her breath with a chuckle.

"Yeah, yeah, Patrick. Most definitely." V. crosses his arms over his chest, sticking his hands under his hairy armpits. "Just waiting for the sun to get off it," he stammers. "You know what they say about cutting the grass in the sun."

"I don't, actually," my father snorts, "except that some people, like me, get a sunburn. But you wouldn't, would you, Al, given your ancestry and all that." My father can be very mean to Italians when he's angry. "Well, you're dressed for it, so I figure you must be planning to do it sometime." My father stands suddenly taller on the sidewalk, and V. shifts from one leg to the other. My father wears an old shirt to mow the lawn, but never just an undershirt like V. has on. And he's scowling at V.'s undershirt.

"Don't wait too long, Al," he says. "Don't you wait here too long yourself, Maria. It's nice to be neighborly, but I think Elda needs some help with the sewing." He parts the traffic angrily as he walks back across the street.

Maria stands up to be sure my father's really leaving. I'm left sitting on the swing alone. She and V. watch my father walk home. "Look at the way that weeping willow caresses your house in the breeze," V. purrs to Maria. "We haven't had a breeze like that in days."

That's how he does it. He says certain words so easily, like "potent" and "caress," turning everything, even the tree, all sexy. He was caressing Maria's eyelids, and now, when he says the word out loud, it gives you goose bumps, just at a moment when you think you've recovered yourself.

"V.," laughs Maria, "you are one slippery fellow with your words. You're the only man I've ever met who makes the weather so damn interesting." She's close enough that her body is almost touching his.

I start to become angry with them for ignoring my father and for ignoring me, and I think they're going too far and should stop. I have to do something, like drop the lemonade. But that would make such a mess. I could fall off the seat. But then I'd just look stupid. What I really want to do is to sit V. down and jump all over him and have him caress my eyelids while Maria has to be the one to think of a way to stop us. They seem to forget I'm here, with their whispers and giggles and little touches all over. Glaring at them, I run my finger up and down the sweat on the lemonade pitcher and then around the rim of one of the stemmed glasses so it lets out a high-pitched squeak.

They're both startled. "Why don't you pour yourself a glass, honey?" Maria asks in a trembling kind of voice.

"C'mon, Al," his mother calls from inside their screen door. I wonder how many people have been watching the two of them. "You need to bring in the rubbish cans so you'll have done something around this place today." Then she stares at my aunt and me. "Not that I blame you, Al, with the two sexiest girls in the neighborhood to..." She pauses. "...drink lemonade with." His mother can do it too—fill words like "lemonade" with frissons. Well, that's probably how he learned the technique.

After that Saturday, cuz we don't actually get back until well over an hour after my father asked us to come home, Aunt Maria and I are banned from visiting the Vieris. My father says we're not even allowed to think about Mr. V. and that we'll be in big trouble if he hears us talking about him. He keeps muttering something about a "damn wolf of a guinea who can't be trusted in the hen house."

So we can only see V. in church. One Sunday we run into him while walking home from Mass, and Maria asks V. if he'll fix her radio that keeps shorting out. He glances at my father, who nods but still gives off an air of disapproval. My father brings the radio to the Vieris' that afternoon, and V. says that he'll rewire it and bring it back in the evening. I'd have much preferred to watch V. fix the radio and see how much frisson he could put into connecting the wires, but I know my father won't let us. So I decide to go to the pool with Agnes and Donna to remind myself what guys my own age look like.

On our walk home from the pool, we don't even stop for a Popsicle cuz it's getting late and I'm angry and embarrassed. I carry all my pool things in a wicker bag that looks like one of Aunt Anna's and I usually love it. But today it feels all scratchy against me.

"I think that boy with the long blue trunks is really cute," moons Agnes. "His blonde hair is going to be so light and streaky by the end of the summer. And I'll bet he's got something really big inside those shorts."

I glower at her. She laughs. "Might just think about 'opening my lips' to him, Bridey."

"Come on, Ag. The guys at the pool are so lame. They're just horny dicks with pimples." One boy tried to pull off my bathing suit bottom after I dove off the high dive, but I haven't told Donna or Agnes. I took in mouthfuls of water getting him away from me at about ten feet under, and when I surfaced, I was choking so much that I had to stop swimming for the rest of the afternoon. The idiot wasn't even supposed to be in the diving area.

"And," I add, "can't you see how immature they are? They laugh when they see girls—they can't even talk to us. They just try to check if our nipples are showing when we come out of the water cuz it's so friggin' cold."

"What's up with you?" sneers Agnes. "You on the rag or something?"

I catch myself. "Sorry. I just wish I could meet someone...you know...not like Edward."

I'm sort of dating Edward cuz he's the only boy who's asked me out. He's a mouth-breather and talks through his nose. He has such a lack of frisson that when my parents first met him, my father actually laughed. He pulled me into the kitchen and told me that I could see Edward whenever I wanted, and he would never worry about me. When I asked what he meant, he said that Edward was so ugly and seemed so unintelligent that we would only refer to him as a "practice boyfriend." I was mortified. If my father made fun of Edward, what would kids my own age say? I try to have our dates at the movies, where we don't have to talk, and at theaters that are far enough away that I'm not likely to see anyone I know. Only Agnes and Donna are aware that I'm even going out with Edward. And I'm not really.

When I get home from the pool, Aunt Maria tells me V. called to say he's fixed her radio. He'll be over in two hours. Which is not that much time for me to get ready. I wash my hair three times with my favorite shampoo and then decide to use it all over my body cuz I certainly don't want to smell like chlorine for V. I put on my shortest pair of hot pants. If my mother says anything, I can remind her that she bought them for me. I also wear my white ribbed T-shirt—the one where my nipples show through when I wear my Olga T-shirt bra.

I make sure that I'm near the door when V. rings the bell. "I'll get it," I call, running down the apartment stairs so we can have a few extra seconds together without anyone noticing.

When I open the door, V. puts his hand on the frame, close to my chest. "Hello, gorgeous." He always says that to me and to just about every other female except his mother. No frisson in that greeting. But then I look at him, holding his stare the way he's often held mine, the way he's been holding Aunt Maria's. I send out frissons like I'm the only one in all of Cambridge who has them to give. V. shuts the outside door.

He puts the radio down and moves closer to me and I don't move back. His arms gently go around me, one behind my neck and one down low on my back, just above the waistband of my hot pants. I stop myself from moving toward him so I won't look too aggressive. I just wait while he slowly draws me closer to him and touches his lips to mine. His tongue steals into my mouth, so softly, and then he pushes against me lightly and then with a little more firmness. I push against him and kiss back, but he's already moving away from me.

It's over. So fast.

I smile at him and he gives me a grin that's disappointingly neighborly. "Let's go up so I can show Maria how well her radio works," he says, readying himself, I know, for giving out more frissons, but not to me.

There must be a look a girl has after a really good kiss—not after an incompetent, slobbering, smelly one, like the kisses I get from Edward— because my father can somehow tell, you know? Not that V. rubbed his palm over my left nipple, which is still tingling; not that V. gently glided my body toward him and pushed his frisson against me. He isn't aware of any of the specifics, but he seems to know all of the generals.

So Mr. V. became even more off-limits to me. When Aunt Maria is allowed to visit him again, I can't go with her. I think of how I waited on his porch while he complimented Maria on her bedroom eyes, knowing my eyes are better than hers any day. And I rehearse what I'd say in confession if V. and I could have the time we need to ourselves, and Aunt Maria would sit on the porch for hours and hours while I was the one who had the bedroom eyes. But I never have any q.t. lovemaking with V. to confess, no matter how often I think about it.

One particularly hot day, when the Vieris are on vacation and I'm sitting on a beach chair in our backyard trying to read *The Catcher in the Rye* for school—I'm so tired of boys' adventures—Aunt Maria comes out. She sits on a beach chair next to me, lights a cigarette, and pulls her dress up to her thighs. "Isn't it hot, Bridget?"

"Yes," I say and offer to get her a cold washcloth.

"No, honey," she says. "You just sit there. There's only one thing that could help how I'm feeling." She looks right into me, her eyes glistening and narrowed just a tiny bit, just that V. bit, just that bedroom-eyes bit.

"You know what could cool me off right now?" she asks, still glaring at me with her feet halfway up the lounge, her knees exposed, fanning her dress back and forth.

I smile but am afraid to say anything. Surely V. wouldn't have told her about our kiss.

"A nice glass of lemonade."

She knows. So I put my feet halfway up the lounge chair too. I do my best to squint my eyes into bedroom eyes. And then we both laugh. She takes a deep drag of her cigarette, and I think how I should be smoking too. We're both thinking about V. and his frissons.

But suddenly she sits up, puts her feet on the ground, and becomes stern. "Bridget," she says in a voice she's never used with me before, "you need to start drinking your lemonade out of another pitcher."

I try to stare at her in wide-eyed innocence, but the sun's too bright and it hurt my eyes. I want to look puzzled but I'm shocked at the cleverness of her metaphor. I begin to wonder if maybe V.'s frissons can even stimulate your brain.

Aunt Maria lights another cigarette from the tip of her last one, and her eyes aren't bedroom eyes now. This is woman-to-woman. "Bridget," she says before another drag, "what I'm doing may be wrong, but honey, what you're just thinking about is dangerous. And do you even bother to consider your mother?"

How can a person smoke the way Aunt Maria does and be able to say that much in one breath? And my mother? What's she got to do with it? She's not in the frisson line as far as I can tell.

"Your mother has done all she can to convince your father that you're Miss Innocence personified," Maria says.

"My mother knows?" I ask, feeling like I'm going to throw up.

"D'you think she's blind?" Maria hisses. Then, more softly, she says, "We can all tell how hot you are for him."

My face is burning. I want to launch into a speech of great indignation, but I can't think how to start.

Not that I could've said anything anyway, cuz Maria's launched into a non-stop lecture. "Bridget, you have your whole life. You'll be the first girl in our family to go to college. You'll meet college boys. Do you really want to go there all dirty from V.? And if your father finds out, you can probably kiss college good-bye, which might just leave you kissing old V. longer than you planned. And probably a lot longer than I'll be kissing him."

I laugh a little fake laugh, and then I realize it isn't so fake. "V.? Yeah, he's kinda sexy for an old guy, but those blackheads and that belly are a turn-off, know what I mean?"

Aunt Maria looks shocked, suspicious, and relieved all at the same time.

"There's this lifeguard at the pool," I start. It's only at that moment I realize he's been giving out frissons to me. Sometimes I can be so slow. "We've been working on our dives together, and..." I don't really know what to tell Aunt Maria cuz I haven't said much more to him than "Hi, Dave," or "Good dive."

"Well," interrupts Aunt Maria, "that's great. I'll bet he's real cute. Clean from all that swimming. And probably has good strong muscles."

"Yeah," I say. "Definitely." 'Course I haven't actually noticed.

"Hey, girl," Aunt Maria says, her tone completely different. "How about going shopping for a new bathing suit? You know, one that you can change into when you're sunbathing after all your diving practice."

I'm astonished. Aunt Maria never has any extra money. "That'd be great," I say, imagining myself in the orange bikini I've been eyeing at Filene's Basement. Even though my mother prefers me to wear one piece bathing suits.

"Well, let's go then," she says, putting her cigarette out on the lawn, something my father hates. "I'll just let your mom know."

She turns back to me as she's pushing the screen door open. "Don't tell your dad about the bathing suit. He'll kill us." Then she gives me a huge smile. "But not as much as he'd have killed old 'bedroom eyes.'"

Poor V., I think. He's only been on vacation for two weeks, and he's lost both of us.

Aunt Maria is back in a moment. "Your mom says to have a good time shopping."

As we walk to the bus stop, Aunt Maria squeezes my clammy hand with hers. "Hey, you know what's best about shopping?"

"No."

"The air conditioning!"

Our eyes catch again. I can see that V. hasn't lost her after all and I look away. Aunt Maria is a lot smarter than I realized.

I put my sweaty arm around her sweaty back. "Yeah," I say, hoping she can tell that I approve of her and V. "That sounds great."

15. I Feel Like I'm On Pretty Good Terms with The Virgin Mary, Even Though I Haven't (So Far) Gotten Pregnant in High School

A lot of the older girls in St. Michael's High School for Girls have had babies—and, like Mary, out of wedlock—so wasn't Mary just so lucky that her baby actually turned out to be the second person of the Holy Trinity. The chances of that are, literally speaking, exactly one to every other person who's ever been born or will be born on earth, know what I mean? I suppose the odds could be changed to three to everyone else if the Father and the Holy Spirit decided to be born again too. 'Course they won't. Anyone can see their personalities wouldn't allow them to be so physical. The "word made flesh" is just not where they're at.

Finding out that Mary's baby was God must have caused her neighbors to stop gossiping (at least publicly) for fear of what He might do to their own kids. The parishioners at St. Michael's could take a lesson from them. There's no way her parents would've threatened to throw her out, like the parents of the older sisters of three girls in my freshman class did. Or that her boyfriend, Joseph, would beat her up, which happens way too often when the boyfriends of St. Michael's girls find out they're going to become fathers. Or, the absolute worst, that her mother gets so frantic about what the neighbors will think that an aneurysm pops in her head, and she falls to the floor and dies right then and there, and it's your fault, and you'll go to hell, and the Blessed Mother won't even care because, by prematurely becoming a mother yourself, you didn't honor your own mother.

None of us could believe when Debbie, a really innocent and fairly malnourished-looking girl, suddenly discovered herself to be "with child," that her own mother would actually die. Poor Debbie. She was so skinny that, at five months, she wasn't even showing. Talk about guilt. That and everyone saying, "You killed your mother," like Debbie could control her mother's blood flow. She didn't have divine powers. She just had sex.

Other girls and their parents at St. Michael's deal with pregnancy in what is clearly a more effective, if slightly sinful, way: they lie. The girls' parents put an announcement in the parish newsletter that their daughter and the guy have been secretly married for a year, but because they were so young when they married, despite the full consent of both sets of parents (and, often, grandparents as well), they couldn't publicize the marriage. So the baby is not only legitimate but, since they're Catholic, to be expected. Cuz everyone knows that worse than having premarital sex is using birth control. It all ends up making sense, and everyone is relatively happy, even if a few dates have to be tweaked.

And the BVM is sort of the patron saint of all the St. Michael pregnant girls since she, herself, got pregnant out of wedlock. I mean, now that we're in high school, they're teaching us that the real Catholic belief about Mary is that she got pregnant through her ear—that "Just as Eve listened to Satan and gave birth to sin, so Mary listened to Gabriel and became pregnant with the Son of God."

Yuck. You have to admit that anatomically, this ear business rivals my father's fear that a bicycle seat could ruin your virginity, know what I mean? The only non-gross thing about the whole ear pregnancy is the realization of how incredibly on-target Agnes was for seeing how central Eve is to everything and how God-the-F repeatedly creates love triangles. I mean, first it's Eve, Adam, and Him. Then it's God-the-F, Gabriel, and Mary. Or God-the-F, Joseph, and Mary. And finally and forever, it's every married woman, her husband, and Him. So, apart from Debbie's mom, the fact that Mary was with child before she and Joseph had a chance to get married (even secretly) is no big deal to anyone in our parish. Many of the young mothers of St. Michael's make special vigils to Mary, expecting that she'll understand their plight. I love the Blessed Mother too, even though I haven't (so far) gotten pregnant in high school.

Because Mary, a female, is so important to Catholicism, you feel that no one should be disappointed by having a girl instead of a boy, or if they are, they might just discover one day what a big mistake they made. Mary showed the world that girls shouldn't be underestimated. And since we always seem to be in every possible way, as I've discovered, she's a real comfort.

Not to mention that it does God the world of good to have Mary in the picture, just from a PR standpoint. If we're going to be brutally honest, the Trinity is a pretty abstract notion. Understanding it is like thinking about the infinity of the universe. Sort of there and not there in a time-space continuum. But once you get a woman into the picture, and a mother, well, it humanizes God, doesn't it? You can connect to Him, knowing He had a mother.

Agnes even points out, one day when we were sentenced to detention for skipping gym and were supposed to say the whole rosary three times (totally unrealistic, since gym is only 35 minutes) before we came out of the locker room, that if you compare the words of the "Hail Mary" with those of the "Our Father," you can see that Mary is so much more "of the people" than He is.

"Blessed art thou among women." Who can't relate to a line like that? It's just saying you're one holy chick and everyone, even God, is totally into you. Put that next to "Thy will be done on Earth as it is in heaven." Oh, come on. First off, He's bossy—and bossy across that nebulous time-space thing.

Agnes says He sounds exactly like her father—and mine too and probably a lot of other fathers—who act like they want everyone to do their will any time, any place. And we're sick of it. We need a female who's relatively normal.

Just before Sister Angelicina comes in and gives us a double Saturday detention for talking rather than saying the rosary, Agnes, who is really warming to the topic, which Sister Angelicina might have recognized if she wasn't so narrow-minded, says she thinks Mary is a kind of biblical Audrey Hepburn, friendly and warm, who'd stare right into your eyes when she talked to you. Unlike all the males, like St. Alphonse Liguori or St. Charles Borromeo, who look constipated or like they have a load in their pants.

And Mary has a favorite color—a really pretty blue. Christ, how ordinary is that? Anyone can relate, even if their own favorite color is brown or some disgusting shade of purple that looks like the color of organs in the science museum. The important thing is that Mary took the time to choose and somehow managed to get it recorded so that all of us girls would know she isn't too high and mighty not to be into colors.

And now that we're finally in high school, what we discover about Mary only gets better and better. She not only likes blue. She likes clothes and her fashion sense is to die for. In our religious art class, we learn that Mary posed for more painters than virtually any other person who ever lived.

She started with St. Luke, who knew so much about her most intimate details, he must have had a thing for her, but I'm sure she didn't realize it cuz she wasn't the type to cheat on Joseph. And then, after that, you can really see that she had an eye for art since she started time-traveling to sit for much better painters than Luke, especially the Italian ones, and her dresses are so beautiful and not all of them blue either. I mean, sometimes they're color-coordinated with the wings of the Angel Gabriel on the day when he came to give her the happy news about her bun in the oven.

Talk about "studied casual" or "dress for success." It's like she could see into the future and know in the morning that it was going to be a day that required maroon brocade. All the Bible stories suggest her house was small, but it must have had some kind of basement closet space cuz—and here you just have to think of Audrey Hepburn again—she has the right outfit for any occasion. And she always knows what to wear. It could have even been a cedar closet like Aunt Anna has. After all, they are native to the area. Cedars of Lebanon, as the Bible says.

As beautiful as she is, you know, too, that Mary was a good girl, except for just the one time (and who knows how any of us would respond to an angel—I mean a real one, not some horny idiot like Timmy Pease that Debbie got involved with). And if I ever did get in trouble, I hope I'd find someone like

Joseph, who's the type of guy my grandmother would call "a good egg." So what's not to like about the BVM? The Mother of God. Good-looking. Well-dressed. A good person. Knows how to make the absolute best of a situation. And never uppity about any of it.

Mary is also into making appearances, what Sister Angelicina tells us we should call "apparitions." At first I felt these were a bit show-offy cuz they flaunted her ability to time-travel. Also I don't think she should have left her family quite so often. But when she isn't dropping in on famous painters, she frequently appears to children, with a higher percentage of girls.

I like that—mixed groups with girls dominating. The kids are usually playing together in some town in Europe or South America that really needs the kind of money her appearance can kick off. A shrine requiring builders who've been out of work. A well that needs diggers to make it deep, and priests and nuns to make it Christian, to bless the water, and to collect the entrance fees. A commemorative spot, perhaps with flowers, around which flourish bed and breakfasts, tea or coffee shops, stores selling relics of every kind—prayer books, holy cards, medals, and statues—most run by locals, helping tourism along again.

On Fridays we spend some of our mornings with Sister Loretta, who says she's named after Our Lady of Loreto (never mind the spelling error). Loreto is a miraculous place in Italy where Mary not only appeared but where her own original house in Nazareth time-travelled to and now can actually be visited over there in Europe!

Sister Loretta shows us her enormous collection of silver and bronze Blessed Virgin medals, most of which she says are related to Loreto in some way. I have two favorites. One is a big silver medal with the

BVM praying over an airplane. I hadn't realized that when Mary was acting as Our Lady of Loreto, she's the patron saint of pilots (which Sister Loretta's brother is—hence her interest) and of all who fly. Talk about keeping up with the modern world. Think about all the time between when Mary lived on earth and when planes were invented. There's no reason she has to take an interest in what we're inventing today, especially since she must be influenced a lot by God-the-F who's so stuck in the past with his Eve obsession. Nothing forward-looking about Him.

My other favorite medal features Mary as Our Lady of the Sword, in which she's depicted as killing pagans. Sister Loretta always brings a big magnifying glass with the medals to help us make out the details more clearly and often to see bits of prayers written in foreign languages on the back. One Friday she lets me take the Lady of the Sword medal over to the window with the magnifying glass so I can try to read some really tiny print that none of us could decipher.

"It's in English," I call out as it comes into focus. "It says 'Made in China.'" At first Sister Loretta thinks I must be wrong, but when she sees the words for herself, she explains to us that God anticipated that the Communists in China would create technology that makes medals, rosaries, and plastic figurines really cheaply, and He was ready to temporarily forgive them for not being a democracy and for being pagans if they were willing to sell these holy goods to us at a fantastic discount, which shows us that God, like everyone else, goes out of His way to get a good deal on something He really needs. Who doesn't like a bargain?

Agnes and Lucy and I are all painting our nails a pale blue in honor of the Feast of the Annunciation on March 25th. We're also avoiding our review for the Diocesan exam the following morning. Diocesan exams are given at the end of March to students in Catholic schools throughout Massachusetts from the fourth to the twelfth grade. You have to answer four out of seven essay questions. A typical question goes something like this:

Theologians speculate about whether Christ actually appeared to His disciples after He rose from the dead. Is the scripture clear on this? Discuss, with reference to the different gospels and their variations, and to different theological interpretations.

Short of traveling the time-space continuum to get interviews with some of the more loquacious disciples, memorizing the Bible, or learning about "theological interpretations"—whatever they are—we're doomed. Doomed to failure by every single one of the seven questions on the exam.

On the test day the exams appear in a tightly sealed envelope on each nun's desk. The envelope can only be opened in the presence of Mother Superior, which leads to significant delays in the test-starting process. Everyone is nervous. Some fart a lot. Others, like my friends and me, just roll our eyes. A few nut jobs finger their rosary beads. "Good luck!" I think. We'll take the exams, do miserably, get yelled at, but at least know they're over for another year.

But this year one Diocesan exam question bothers me a lot. It's about the Blessed Virgin herself. "I recommend that you all answer Question Five," Sister Angelicina states sternly.

5. *Our Lady has blessed children all over the world by appearing to them. Today she has chosen to appear to you alone. Describe, step-by-step, what your words and actions would be with the Blessed Mother—particularly what you would say to Her while in Her presence and then what you*

178

would do after Her visit to preserve Her memory, carry out Her wishes, etc.

Out of all of the hundreds of kids in St. Michael's school taking the horrid test, I'm the only one foolish enough, fearful enough, obedient enough, and stupid enough to actually try to answer Question 5.

As I read the question over and over, my whole body begins to sweat. What if the Virgin appeared to me? It's all well and good her showing up in Fatima or Loreto or Walsingham or remote places we've never heard of. But if I looked up and saw her, perhaps slightly translucent, floating around the picnic table in my backyard, I would, no questions asked, run like hell until I couldn't see her anymore. Why would the Virgin appear to me? Yes, I show her love and devotion and feel her presence, but I'm not expecting to actually meet her on the street or anything.

"Go away! Our economy is fine here in the greater Boston area. I think they need you in Peru." My mother would have an embolism and die if she saw the Virgin or saw me seeing her. I'd be like Debbie, except it would be the Virgin who murdered my mother, not me. But who'd believe that? I'm breathing really fast. Sister Angelicina comes over to me. I think she's a little afraid I might actually be having a vision. I should say I am, and maybe I could get out of the exam.

I have to collect myself. This is a test. All I have to do is write something that sounds plausible. And religious. And normal. Not "I'd run like the devil!" Not "I'd shriek to her to go away!" Not "I'd implore Her to explain why on earth She'd chosen me." So I try to picture the Virgin in her lovely dresses, especially in the portraits she had painted in Italy. Slide after slide that we studied in Religious Art. Red silk. Blue brocade. Green velvet. I breathe in and out slowly, imagining, with increasing tranquility, the feel of those beautiful fabrics in my hands and against Mary's body. I see her, serene, as the Archangel Gabriel gives her tidings of the great joy to come. Peaceful, as her pregnancy begins to show, sitting in exquisite maternity dresses with her mother, St. Anne, or her ladies in waiting. And then composed and maybe a little proud as she holds the baby Jesus on her lap.

My mind goes back to the day we discussed the Da Vinci Annunciation. Mary is resplendent in a pale-red silk empire-styled dress, gathered right under the breasts with a blue velvet ribbon. Her wrap, a sumptuous blue silk lined with gold satin, covers one shoulder, her lower body, and trails along the tiles of her terrace, where she's reading. I ask Sister why, while Mary's slender right fingers holds down the page of the bit in Isaiah that talks about her, her left arm is raised up, palm forward, suggesting surprise or even a desire to protect herself from Gabriel, to stop his message. Sister shrieks, "Stop talking, Bridget!" inadvertently putting her left arm up, palm forward, as Mary had, crying out that I'm a blasphemer and that my classmates should block their ears so my words can't endanger their souls as they are surely blackening my own.

I stop speaking but I also stop listening to her— only vaguely hearing threats of Saturday detentions—and go back to looking at that slide. Mary's eyes gaze at Gabriel, but she seems to want to get back to her book. Her lips purse slightly, I think in disapproval of having her reading interrupted. "Wonderment," Sister said, which was what led me to raise my hand in the first place. It isn't just amazement that an angel is in her garden. The slight tilt of her head, her expression, her lips, her eyes, her hand, all suggest polite resistance to Gabriel's disclosure. She's weighing her options.

In detention, Sister asks me to talk about why I would want to even imply that Mary was anything less than an obedient servant of the Lord her God, why I raised doubts for the whole class about Mary's awe at being told she was to become the Mother of God. I try to explain that I'm not suggesting how Mary really felt but only how she looks in the painting. I have to clap the erasers out the window and wash the blackboards for three weeks every day after school with soap and water. Sister tells me that perhaps cleaning blackboards will remind me that I need to clean my soul as well as my mind and evil tongue.

Now, staring at Question 5, I realize that Sister was right. My reaction to the idea of Mary's appearing to me resembles what I'd said was her own reaction to the Angel Gabriel. She sees Gabriel and, dressed in red silk and blue satin, with a lovely view of Florence from her garden, says, "No! Go have the baby yourself."

So maybe Mary didn't want to have a child. And suddenly she's there in another slide, breast-feeding Him in a light-green satin dress. I can tell, from the look on her face, she feels that parenting Jesus is, after all, no picnic. I mean you have a baby, and it turns out to be God. Where does that leave her? She can't even discipline Him. And talk about on-demand feeding. He's God, for heaven's sake. What He wants, He has to be given. Her breasts were probably bleeding, never mind His Sacred Heart.

She must have been so chapped and exhausted and overwhelmed. And what did she do during the terrible twos? How long did it take to toilet train Him? Did she believe in spanking? And if she did, you probably don't hit the Son of God on his bottom, even lightly, even if He's been a cranky brat all day. Could she send Him to bed without His supper?

No wonder she often left her family on a whim to whisk off to have her nine thousandth portrait painted in some later century. Oh God. I don't want to think these things, though I see they're probably true. Poor Mary. Why didn't she run like hell? Of course she probably did, but who stands a chance against an angel who can fly? Who stands a chance against your own child when He turns out to be God?

So she's allowed to have a favorite color. She gets to time-travel to visit painters and become famous across all time and space. But not primarily to honor her son. She just wants a few hours away from Him. She must have been so harried. The painters probably made her look more beautiful than she actually was since they were hoping to sell the painting for a good price, and they were depicting the Mother of God, after all. So even if she looked like crap, sweating, her hair not washed recently, her clothes stained in baby puke, they had to make her attractive.

And then I have another awful realization. She didn't get to keep the clothes.

And then more terrible. They weren't her clothes.

And worse still. There were no clothes. The artists had pieces of fabric lying around their studios to get them started with a painting. When Mary appeared to each of them, she'd look sad and tired and so disappointed in how her life had turned out. She'd be wearing her faded blue, mended, layered-enough-so-they-weren't-see-through old clothes. The painters, motivated not by God but by greed, draped her with a piece of fabric or put her in some other woman's dress and totally recreated her with vivid palettes and even more vivid imaginations.

And then a fly would land on her nose, and she'd give it a quick rub. And the painter would scream at her, "Mother of God! Can't you hold still for ten minutes? Ten minutes. That's all I ask."

And ten minutes is all I have left for Question 5. I've learned a lot about Mary and about myself, but I realize it's one of those situations where "the test isn't capable of measuring the test taker's abilities." We had a whole discussion of those kinds of tests after there was a piece on them in the *Globe*. 'Course Sister Angelicina said there's no such thing, that it's just a fancy term for poor performance. For her, there's only students who don't study sufficiently or aren't bright enough. But she's wrong.

I pick up my pen and begin to write as fast as I can. I say that if Mary appeared to me, I'd kneel down and start saying "Hail Marys" (that is so totally lame!) and that I'd look down so that my eyes weren't blinded by her halo. She doesn't get a chance to talk much in my essay. I'm too busy praying at her. Eventually I invite her back to my house to look at my holy card collection and the statue of her and St. Anne that my mother bought in white porcelain and painted herself. Anne's outfit is brown and organ red. Finally (even more desperately), I write that she looks at her watch—which, of course, is absurd cuz people at that level of the holy hierarchy don't need watches. She says, "Bless you, my child," and strokes my cheek with a soft and gentle hand. I ask if she wants me to set up a pilgrimage site, though in fact our block is pretty crowded with three-family houses. She says no. I suggest a small holy store and even offer to sell some of my precious touched to a relic holy cards, the only ones I have left after burying my indulgence ones on the q.t. back in the fifth grade. I also offer her my glow-in-the-dark saints (also made in

China). But she says no. And then she vanishes. My apparition—like my essay—is a total bust.

I still haven't filled even one page. I bite on the end of my pen, pretty sure that I'll fail this question, but figuring I said enough to escape excommunication. So I decide I can write my last paragraph for her and not the test givers.

Mary didn't even get to keep the clothes, and that is perhaps the least of the offenses committed against her. Her sorrow is so deep. Everyone asks too much of her. She is just a woman caught in God's world. She is trapped in a domestic situation that is not of her own making. She didn't have a chance to write her own story. It's been men who have written it and, as usual, they have elevated her so long as she could be thought of as the Virgin—compliant, meek, obedient, cooperative, and humble.

I predictably do quite poorly on the test, which is totally immaterial to me, but unfortunately not to my parents or my teachers or to Sister Superior. I have to wash blackboards for the rest of the year. But I hardly mind cuz in writing that paragraph and in the innumerable times I read it and try to explain it to my parents, to various nuns, to Sister Angelicina, to Sister Superior and most embarrassingly, to Bishop O'Brien, who summons me for a private audience, I realize that I might understand Mary more than I ever imagined. And that while I'm not expecting her or the Archangel Gabriel to appear to me, others will appear—like Satan, the Ellises, Uncle Michael, or even V.—with messages and demands. Others against whom pursed lips, a disapproving gaze, and even a raised left arm, palm forward, will be insufficient defense.

Holy Mary, blessed art thou among women. Thank you for visiting me—without actually appearing—on that exam day. Thanks for the warning. And for your support. I promise I'll try to defend myself. I'll get a driving license, but I won't threaten to leave my husband and child(ren). I won't have to. I'll become educated and maybe even a businesswoman, but I won't marry a man who'll steal from me. And I won't pretend the way you, Our Lady, were stuck having to pretend or the way Santa Anna does. No fake twenties. No Joseph on the side. I open myself to you and to all women—dead or alive, Catholic or pagan—who will help me to be strong, whether they're giving me grace, advice, or cootras.

⌘

Acknowledgments

I'm not sure that I ever would have started writing this book were it not for Joe Gibaldi who, well over a decade ago, having discovered that I was half Italian and a decent story teller, remonstrated that it was my duty to "come out" as an Italian American both to the Modern Language Association and to the world. Regardless of what my religious beliefs were at the time, Joe relied on my Catholic upbringing to ensure I'd follow his counsel and his extensive reading list.

I am deeply grateful to Edvige Giunta who encouraged my writing, putting me, year after year, on panels at Italian American conferences, and introducing me to a community of Italian American scholars, storytellers, performance and visual artists, and filmmakers, so many of whom have been supportive of my work and from whom I've learned so much. I pay many of you the highest tribute I can: I teach your work.

While I was writing individual stories, I was happy enough writing memoir. But when it came time to link these stories more tightly, I found memoir constraining and fiction to be quite liberating. So while *Dodging Satan* is "based on true stories," it has been fictionalized.

Early versions of chapters have appeared in the *South Carolina Review*, *Witness*, *Calyx*, *Fugue*, *Italian Americana*, *Willow Review*, *Tiny Lights*, *Kestrel*, *Phoebe*, *The Rambler*, *Rock and Sling*, *A River and Sound Review*, and *Zone 3*.

I want to thank Stephanie Acton who photocopied those early pieces I was sending to journals, back when submissions had to be paper rather than electronic. One day I walked by her office and stopped because I thought she was crying.

She was, in fact, simply laughing very hard, reading one of my stories. I hadn't even realized she'd grown up Catholic. Stephanie was one of the first people who read my work and she encouraged me more than she realized.

When I interviewed for my job at Purchase College, SUNY, our Assistant Dean, Rich Nassisi, said at dinner, "Purchase changes lives." This is usually understood in relation to our students. But Purchase has also changed my life significantly. The creativity of my colleagues and students has inspired me—on almost a daily basis. There are too many of you to name, but I hope you know how grateful I am to work or to have worked with you. And I especially want to thank my Learning Community students.

My deepest debt is to my husband, Gary Waller, a fine Renaissance and medieval scholar and the man who daily still demonstrates to me that a good marriage doesn't ever involve the "enmity" that, as a child, I read about in the Bible, continually witnessed in my and my friends' families, and that, for a while, I believed could only be escaped by becoming a nun.

In the 80s, when we were all—heady with reading Derrida, Barthes, and Lacan—reveling in the notion of our split subjectivities, our multiple selves, Gary informed me that one of my selves was clearly a "parish Catholic." Having been educated by Jesuits and being the junior Joycean in a large and quite prestigious English department, I didn't take kindly to that remark, though it was, of course, annoyingly spot on, and is really the bedrock of this book.

Our work, though very different, has had multiple confluences—pedagogy, Cultural Studies, and most recently, the Virgin Mary. While Gary engages in scholarship on the intellectual and psychological power of the stories surrounding the Virgin Mary—whether in art or writing, whether in "sacred" texts or contemporary popular accounts of "BVM sightings", I'm writing about my childhood beliefs in Mary's time traveling to have her portrait painted, on questions of how she parented, and on her amazing wardrobe. But the joy in traveling in Italy, France, and the UK, whether to see a single Pontormo in a small church near Florence or to Marian sites such as Walsingham, has been multiplied by our joint interests in Mary and by the pleasure of meeting fellow travelers.

My stepsons, Michael and Andrew, and our son Philip—all so creative in their own pursuits—must be acknowledged for their love, their example, and their fond interest. I want especially to thank Philip who sat through numerous readings of my work, even in those teenage years when it's particularly hard for kids to find their mother's jokes funny. With great generosity of spirit, Philip *always laughed*. Most specifically, I am grateful for Philip's insisting that I write about my childhood belief in what "the holy" in holy water actually was.

I am grateful to Tory Hartmann, my editor at Sand Hill Review Press, for insightful comments, keeping me to the deadlines, and seeing this project through. I also want to thank fellow Sand Hill writers, including James Hannah and especially Nanci Lee Woody for her wit, advice, and friendship.

⌘

If you enjoyed *Dodging Satan*, we hope you will take time to review the book on Amazon, Kindle, Goodreads or your favorite place to hang out with books and readers!

CPSIA information can be obtained
at www.ICGtesting.com
Printed in the USA
FSHW02n2351171018
52958FS